Whiskey Nipple

Stories

Doug Frelke

REDLINE PRESS
BOSTON MASSACHUSETTS

FIRST REDLINE PRESS EDITION, JANUARY, 2000

Copyright © 2000 by Doug Frelke

All rights reserved under the international and Pan-American Copyright Conventions. Published in the United States by Red Line Press a division of AF Publishing, Boston.

Redline Press and its logo are trademarks of AF Publishing.

Redline ISBN: 0-9677771-1-9

Printed in the United States of America
10 9 8 7 6 5 4 3 2 1

Cover art by paperairline.com

Foreword

In my family, there's an old practice, vaguely Irish, of giving a teething baby a bottle with the nipple rubbed in whiskey. I guess there is some thought that this will quiet the baby, soothe her and by doing so, quiet and soothe the parents as well. No one pretends it aids in the teething – the baby still has to break in her teeth. But it is the best we can offer.

As I was working to finish these seven stories, I kept coming back to that thought: these must be the best I can offer. I've worked on these stories, in some cases, for close to five years. They've been a large part of what I do. I'm sure that it has become a part of life for my writer friends as well: Jo-Ann Graziano, Leslie Macmillan, Joe O'Farrell, Mary Caulfield, Anne Farma – and for my professor, Gretchen Mazur, since they have borne the brunt of every single version of every single story. I appreciate the time away from their own work that this community of writers has offered to me and to my stories.

I hope that you cry when you read these stories, or yell or throw them hard against the wall. I want you to come out having been submerged in these stories. I don't care if you read them in this book or on a subway wall I just want to get them to you.

Doug Frelke
January 2000

Stories

Love Canvas 1

White Dog 8

Push 25

Living With the Magician 54

Smoke 63

El Corazon 81

Sophia Bonita 90

Love Canvas

Wallace has two distinct thoughts; they swing back and forth in his head, as if they are hung from a chain. "I am ugly," he thinks; and, "an artist can be forgiven anything." His own large flat face is reflected in his kitchen window. He has a wart under his left eye and though he shaves it, a hair stands out in a bristle. And Wallace knows he is all bristles and black hair and bad skin and that he is short too, less than five feet standing in his socks. An ugly little dwarf.

Outside, the darkness has come, leaving the grassy roll of his backyard black. Behind the yard, his little black creek; above the yard and creek, the sky is black. He is an artist, so the black of the grass is the black of loneliness, and the water is a shiny reflective tar black. The sky is black like the color of blood in old black and white movies. That is good, he thinks, pleased with himself. He has an eye, as they say, and a hand that can render an object clean and true, "like a picture," they say, and they mean a skilled photographic image. Most of his work is for ad agencies. He draws places he has never been, creating backdrop scenes from old issues of

Doug Frelke

the *National Geographic.*

Robert Johnson sings over four flush mounted Bose speakers, balanced in each corner of the kitchen – "When the train, it left the station/ With two lights on behind."

Wallace has always loved Robert Johnson. And he has always loved his wife, Caroline. He had drawn her the first time he saw her – a gifted rendering, even with just a black ball-point on the inner pages of his *Architectural Drawings* textbook. Caroline had loved it when he had allowed himself to be caught with the drawing. She said he was inspiration and romance – a real artist. Those pages are pressed and mounted now, above his drafting desk.

Wallace feels the cold attacking him through the double paned glass of the huge kitchen window. It is funny – how much time and effort he spent on insulation – R factor nineteen fiberglass in the new walls, beading caulk around the gaps in the exterior where the old house had settled, mounting a new tight skin of extruded plastic siding. He has always prided himself on his precision – measure twice and cut once, whether he is re-hanging a door or thinking out his approach to a canvas. Yet he is cold. And angry that this cold can get into his house, the house he rebuilt for Caroline.

Useless, Wallace thinks. He places his hands on the window, palms three feet apart. Then he leans hard against the glass with all his weight, pushing. The interior pane strains and then finally pops, shooting spidery thin cracks out from his hands to the window edge. "There," he says.

Caroline lies still on their white oak table, behind him in the kitchen. He laid her there because she is five feet, ten inches tall and the table is six feet, ten and a half inches long. He had cut it just short of seven feet to give her a little extra room to navigate around the dark blue enamel oven with its wide steel faced door.

Her neck is a bloom – red finger marks from where Wallace had choked her, with yellow blue bruises rising

Love Canvas

in puffs around the suppressed red skin. The effect gives her whole neck a painted look which appeals to him, though he realizes he should be thinking his wife is dead, that he has just killed his own wife.

After their romance began, Wallace had to leave to spend his final semester at the Sorbonne. He wanted to paint Caroline; something more substantial than his pen drawing – oil and canvas, like Rembrandt or one of the old masters. Wallace dedicated himself to that picture, working late into the night after his classes were done, his Robert Johnson playing loud off a cheap pirated tape and a paint covered boom box.

But Wallace never found the right red for Caroline's hair. He spent weeks painting, mixing in any possible thing – wax and spit, his own blood and semen – leaving the colors in little baby food jars around his studio, noting the ingredients in each batch, waiting to see if the color would age to the desired shade. He always ended by whiting the canvas, hiding his failure.

After a year in Paris, he went back to Caroline and took a job with Walker Stanley painting the scenes behind their ad copy. He has been from the very start, enormously successful – with work in the current issues of *The New Yorker, Cosmopolitan, Forbes*. His best works hang in his studio, mounted in carved mahogany frames and rendered on the finest Japanese paper.

He retrieves an almost full gallon of gasoline from down in the shed; he had planned to burn some leaves as soon as spring came, and use their ashes to feed Caroline's hybrid tea roses. As Wallace comes up the stairs, he remembers an unopened bottle of Glenlivet scotch in the pantry, a Christmas present to himself. He places the gas in the corner, away from the stove. He gets down on his knees and reaches to the back of the pantry for his scotch, past the spinach macaroni and the cotton bags of dried legumes.

He cannot find the glass he wants – none of the tumblers are clean. So he sips the scotch from the bottle, gently, wiping the mouth of the bottle each time

3

Doug Frelke

with his hand. There is plenty of time, he thinks, and that is so stupid he has to catch himself from collapsing into a fit of laughter. "Crazy," he thinks, saying the word out loud.

Wallace places the bottle near Caroline's head and goes out to his studio to fetch his paints and brushes. A five by seven execution of a night scene of the Mozartplatz of Salzburg hangs above his paints – his favorite work. Wallace pulls it from the wall, unsatisfied. He turns it to the light, shifting the painting in his hands. He is sure the work is flawless, that this is his best work, every brush stroke precise. But he does not like this picture anymore.

He leaves the print on the studio floor. There is a Jackson and Perkins rose catalog on his work table, and he picks that up on his way out.

Caroline had introduced him to roses. She loved roses, grew the roses in their yard, agonized over her choices. She had begged him to paint them, and he had tried, thinking of the irises and sunflowers of Van Gogh. He went to the library and checked out picture books of roses, rose histories, horticultural manuals. He learned that seventy percent of all perfumes use rose oil as their base; that there is a strain of rose, called Afferon from Bulgaria that bleeds its fragrance so thickly that it fills the entire valley before the flowers die; that the ancient Egyptians buried their mummies with necklaces of rose; that when Napoleon was on campaign he used to send unique root stock back home to his Josephine. And he sold a few backgrounds using roses. But he never painted a rose that was more than that – a backdrop setting for a new car or a clothing model.

He swallows the scotch, coughs. They had been dressing for Handel's Messiah when Caroline had told him – she was beautiful – her red hair cut short, wearing a velvet dress of Titian red. She could not see his face – he was bent over, trying to find his brown Johnson and Murphy loafers from the floor of his

Love Canvas

closet. When he did not look up, she came closer, asked him if he had anything to say. He waited. She stepped again, nearer; he turned then and caught her. He choked her. He did not quit choking her. That still puzzles him; he does not understand why he did not stop. He should have stopped, become reasonable. Women leave men and men leave women. That's the blues, that's his favorite Robert Johnson. And he knew, he had to have known, really he had to have known. He could hear all the people they knew saying that line over and over – he really must have known. But he had killed her.

He unbuttons her red velvet dress. He is delicate, careful not to snag the material as he slides it off, letting it pile softly on the Mexican tile floor. He removes her slip and her underwear; his fingers slide along the beige silk, the white cotton. They hadn't had sex for some time, almost three months, and so he pauses, caught up in seeing her lying like that, naked and still, which she never was.

He begins, taking his time and working slow. The paint doesn't adhere well, so he dabs the blemishes on her skin with a white primer first. He opens the catalog to the red roses and folds over the page of long stemmed Mr. Lincolns. He paints bouquets of the dark red Mr. Lincolns on each breast, three roses each. He does not paint her neck, since it already has its own full color. Instead, he draws a giant yellow Doubloon as big as a fist in the hollow under her neck.

His hands are lined with the same reds and yellows, as is the top of his bottle of scotch. He touches his own face then, presses his hands against his cheeks. His fingers splay over his eyes and streak his face, like Indian face paint. He smells turpentine, paint, Caroline's perfume.

He paints old-fashioned Parson Pinks on her belly – huge blooms, with flowers that fade fast off the vine. Caroline had liked them, so he planted them close to the house. They have a smell like honey and cut grass and

Doug Frelke

she would open the window to get the scent.

He lifts her pale arms, painting each like turning a length of wood along a lathe. He paints long green vines and rose leaves, buds of exotic colors – blue, magenta, orange – hints of strange cross breeds and impossible shades.

He leaves her legs to last, because he is not sure what to do with them, awaiting inspiration. He starts with her toes, concentrating on each, a little brown root. Her ankles look thicker with the paint, solid, and he starts to add thorns now – as he gets into the rough of her calves. He makes thorns as long as his finger, and he adds a dab of red for blood on the sharpest spears.

He decides to paint her face white. He adds slight grey whorls and pink edges until her face is a rose, the white rose, Alba Capri, Napoleon's favorite.

He steps back. She lies on the table, stiff. He turns on the overhead pocket lights, and they snap on, outlining her hips, her chest, her face. He notices immediately that the rose bouquet on her left breast is much larger than the one he painted on the right; also, the thorns on her legs are rubbed out in places, showing the accidental smears of his hand. He laughs; he is happy. The imperfections make it more real to him, all the more tender and pointed.

Wallace realizes that his CD has stopped. He is not sure for how long, for how many hours silence has held the gap, since it is a peaceful kind of silence, the kind that comes with the quietness of winter and the end of steady noise. He thinks of his favorite Robert Johnson line, from a song called *Kind Hearted Woman Blues* – "She's a kind hearted woman/But she studies evil all the time/You well's to kill me, baby/As to have it on your mind."

Evil and kindness; Wallace never understood what that line meant. He has heard that song at least a hundred times since he was twenty-two, graduating from college half his life ago. At times, he was sure he had finally grasped the meaning, understood the words. But

Love Canvas

he does not know Robert Johnson.

He can admit that now. He still likes the line though, for its heavy broken sound. Wallace restarts the CD, leaving white paint on the stereo where he opens the cabinet. He fetches their camera from the closet and takes pictures of her – with the lights on, with the lights dimmed, different angles, one shot against the black backdrop of the big window. He seals the camera in a plastic baggie to protect it from the snow. He opens the big picture window, aware of the cracked pane, and throws the camera out into the blackness. Someone will find his camera, Wallace knows.

He leaves the window open. He tries to clean his brushes, but the scotch has made him sloppy so he leaves them alone, a small pile of sticks near his paints. He sloshes the gasoline on the white oak table, the mound of her clothes, the Mexican tiles. He takes down his little pen drawing of Caroline. It is one of his smallest works, roughly ten inches by twenty-five, the size of two sheets of paper and a frame. He slides the drawing underneath his arm. He piles the other prints in the middle of his studio and lights the fire. The cracked mahogany frames smoke as the fire takes hold, burning out the paper from beneath the glass.

Wallace returns to the kitchen. He sits under the open window; he is no longer cold. He feels sharp, brassy, alive. Wallace traces his finger over the glass, following the black ball-point lines of his drawing. The fire catches on her dress, causing the velvet to crinkle and flame. Wallace laughs. "Titian red," he says.

White Dog

I have never been good with words. I am nervous, standing on Mrs. Baxter's concrete porch, so I check my uniform in the glass inset of her front door. My bleached collar closes tight around its shined gold buttons; polyester creases snap in straight lines down my shirt, along the cut of my trousers. My white shoes are lit with fresh polish. I look ready: set, and perfect.

Mrs. Baxter's porch is built two-feet off the ground, with an old brown rush mat laid from end to end and a green slider in the farthest corner from the door. Her lawn has been mowed today, cut wet, and so the yard smells of fresh grass and dew mixed with the scent of lunch on the stove, collards and ham. Red geraniums in white cast iron kettles line the front of the porch, so alive that they drip over the concrete edge halfway to the grass.

I wait for Chief Kenney to get the paperwork I left behind in the government vehicle. Our job is all paper, so many times to sign so many names – Sailor's Life, Delta Dental, Dependent Health – we are administrators more than messengers.

I knock on the door. Mrs. Baxter answers. Past her shoulder, I can see her family laid about the sides of her den. She recognizes me – Chief and I had come out here

White Dog

last week to tell her that her husband, Frank, a Boatswainmate on an LTD out of Little Creek, had been swept overboard in a storm off of Hatteras. When we came out that first time, we told her we were still looking for him; the LTD crew with Navy helos and the Coast Guard had their people out, too. But Chief and I knew it was over. Just waiting for someone somewhere to find the body.

But Mrs. Baxter didn't know until she saw me standing on her porch; I am not sure what she believed before then – whether she thought her husband would knock on that door at some point, kiss her, comment on the good job she had done on the lawn. But when she sees me, something in the back of her head shatters; I watch its effect move across her face like a light winking out. She knows.

She says, "I've got some collards on the stove." She turns away, letting the screen door bang against the jamb.

I open the screen to follow her, watch her cross to the stove and lift the aluminum pot cover with her bare right hand. She shoves her left arm into the pot, up to the elbow joint. She looks at me then with her winked out face. By her expression, she appears distracted; a slight upturn at the corner of her mouth, as if she is surprised that she is still able to feel anything. She doesn't scream, but someone else does, and then I know it is me, making loud harsh sounds while her sisters and uncles rush into the kitchen.

What can you do? We are not responsible, as Chief always says. He has said that a hundred thousand times in the six months I have been doing this job with him. He recites the line to me and to himself, like his own little prayer.

I yank the neat folder of paperwork the Chief has so properly prepared from his grasp. I hold it too tightly, creasing the folder. As I approach the family, I drop the whole package, kicking the papers across the den floor.

One of Mrs. Baxter's uncles helps gather it up; he's at least sixty and his teeth are gone, but he still grins at me with his red gums. I explain I need her to sign here, here, and here and he nods, says he will take care of it. He

9

smiles his red gum grin, like he has seen this all before. Chief Kenney gives him his card, says he will call in the morning when she is feeling better.

Chief drives us back to the office, tells me maybe I should take the rest of the day off – these are hard things, hard days, hard truths. He does not say any of that - not really, except about taking off the day. I agree. I have other places to go.

When my Pa asks me, and he always does, I say, "Really, Pa. You look pretty good today." Then I help him into his wheel chair, tucking the corners of his blanket under his hairless thighs. He likes to be pushed out among these long corridors that go on like hills with their rolling depth. There isn't much other family here at the VA hospital in New Bern, North Carolina: a few last wives, a couple of youngest daughters. I come to visit in Navy whites like he used to wear. Only he was enlisted and wore crackerjacks; I wear officer dress whites. Still, a kind of sameness, father to son.

He says, "I do look better today. It's because I feel better, a hell of a lot better." He stretches his arms towards the ceiling. "I really feel like a million bucks today." I nod, but he is talking to himself.

"Go to the left up here. I want you to meet somebody."

"Pa," I say. But I do not argue. He is always meeting somebody.

He puts on his brakes at the nurse's station next to radiology. "Sally, this is my boy, Billy." Sally smiles at him, comes round from behind her desk. She is short, five feet tall or so – his preference. My mother is five foot two.

As Sally walks towards us, bits of hair swing into her eyes and she shoos them away from her face, shaking her head. Her face is freckled, with deep-set hazel eyes and that thick auburn bob that gives her such trouble. He shuffles in his chair until his blanket falls on the floor. "Damn," he says.

Sally doesn't know my Pa or any of his pirate tricks,

White Dog

so she bends over to pick up his blanket.

But he's not as smooth as he used to be, now in this hospital dulled by all the drugs. There is a glimmer in Sally's eyes before she bends, when she is still looking at me, and I think she is on to him. But she plays along, bending, and her white polyester skirt tightens around the curve of her hips. Then she folds the blanket back in around his legs.

"I have to warn you about my Billy boy. He's a wild one. I don't know if I should be introducing the two of you. I don't want you to hold me responsible, Sally." He runs his hands over his head in a ghost move, one I'd seen as a kid, back before the cancer and the chemo, when he'd run his fingers through his old black pompadour.

"He doesn't look that dangerous."

He leans on my arm. "Oh, let me tell you, Sally, let me tell you." She smiles; I smile, too. And he begins to tell her a story, about when I was five and had three girl friends. "You wouldn't believe how rough those little girls could get," he says, and he spins up fights and jealousies. He gets the girls' names wrong, mixes their families. I am not in this story, not in any real way. The truth is he wasn't there either; when I was five he was with the Navy on a six-month cruise of South America. I remember the post cards, my mother showing me the pictures from Quito and Vera Cruz, getting out an old Rand McNally and showing me where he was. My Pa heard the girlfriend story through my mother, either in a letter or on the phone. But to hear him telling Sally you would never know; his words sound so fine.

When he is done, Sally laughs. It is a full laugh, with pretty white teeth. "You are dangerous, Billy," she says.

Sally checks her wrist. "I have to get to the rest of my rounds." She gathers up her clipboard from the desk and heads down the hall, her nurse's shoes squeaking on the linoleum. Then she turns her head, back to me, flashing me that wide smile from under her hair.

My Pa winks at me. He has done this many times before, in other places, and I can already imagine our

11

Doug Frelke

future conversations. He will ask me about Sally, but only as an introduction to his talk about his women; he will tell stories, but none about my mother – he will stay away from the raw, rough spots – leaving out facts whenever necessary.

When I was little and he was home, I used to make him tell me stories. He would tell me about looking for gold in South America and meeting the black princesses of Arabia; but my favorite story was of Blackbeard the Pirate. When he had left my mother and me for good, I would retell that story to myself, playing the whole scene out with shoe boxes and green plastic army soldiers, remembering him. But what I have come to realize is this man with his cancer is not the man I remember. Somewhere within the sixteen years between his stories, a ghost came in and took his place. One I created on that floor, moving around my shoeboxes. And I cannot reconcile this man in front of me with the memories of that ghost I dreamed.

When my Pa died three weeks later, I was driving from the hospital in New Bern back to the Bachelor Officer Quarters in Norfolk. So for the two hours I was driving, my father's death was suspended, while Chief Kenney waited for me in the parking lot of the BOQ. To me, that means he lived two hours longer than if I had been in the next room and walked in to find him dead.

So I always drive slow to a death notification. I'll stop to get a soda, chat up the girl at the counter – I am a delinquent messenger, buying time. Today is Shelby, North Carolina, and Mrs. Rubia Hayden, who is waiting for me to tell her that her husband, Eddie Hayden, was killed when he drove through a red light and into the brick wall of a bank. He died more or less instantly; he had enough alcohol in him that he never felt the steering wheel pierce his lungs. But my problem is that I always want to know the whole story – to the last breath. And I imagine Eddie Hayden, eyes open, confused, just trying to breathe so he can go back to sleep.

White Dog

"Do you think I'm pretty?" Rubia Hayden asks, naked beside me on her cheap brass bed.

"No." I say. I have not thought about her prettiness before, and so I blurt out the truth – Rubia is not an especially attractive woman.

She is tall and rangy and she is older than she owns to – it shows when she walks naked around the room, in the extra fold of her belly, the growing thickness of her thighs. I mark her as middle thirties, though she has told me she is twenty-eight.

Rubia would be plain except for her frizzy yellow-orange hair, which she wears long to the small of her back. It's her natural color, the color of a first struck match, and when you see it against her pale skin and her white sheets, it gives the illusion that she is on fire.

I try to better my answer. "You're not pretty, Rubia. You're gorgeous." I roll the "r" in her name and stretch out the "gorgeous," until it sounds theatrical and luxurious.

"Ha!" Rubia slaps me, hard. "You're just saying that because you fucked me. And now you're feeling guilty." She rolls out of her bed, sliding into a worn pink terry cloth robe. "You shouldn't feel guilty. I fucked you, too. Want another beer?"

"Sure." We have plenty of time. In a few more hours we will get dressed and attend the funeral of her husband. Then I will leave.

When I had arrived to do the notification, Rubia answered the door dressed for work – her hair high up in a bun, wearing a baby blue waitress uniform. We sat on her couch, and I told her. And then she cried.

Rubia untied her waitress apron, dabbed at her eyes with a corner. I offered her a Kleenex. She thanked me, blew her nose. "It's just so surprising, to think of Eddie dead. I spoke to him on his birthday."

"Yes," I said. "He was very young. Only thirty-eight."

She nodded. "I need a drink," she said. She asked me if I would like one. I said that's not really done. Then she said, "I'm going to have a drink and you're going to have

13

a drink. Maybe a couple of drinks."

When Rubia returned with the drinks, she had let her hair down from the bun; I was struck with that hair – three feet of that fire color, all wild knotted kinkiness. I knew then what would happen.

Now Rubia is in the kitchen getting the beer. Her closet door stands open, and among all of her shoes and pocketbooks and her black crepe funeral dress, I see one of Eddie's uniforms, an old set of crackerjacks under plastic. I point them out to her when she comes back. "You should close the door, at least," I say.

"Does it bother you?"

I shrug.

"You're not so tough," she says.

Rubia gives me my beer, sits cross-legged beside me. She says, "You know, there was a time when I thought I might be an actress; back when I was nineteen and out working the tables in Vegas. That's how I met Eddie."

Rubia wears her hair round her shoulders, like a worn Indian blanket. "He was on leave and spending money, losing big at my table every night. Somehow I liked that, the loser in him. Always believing he'd win the next time, getting taken and coming back." She runs her hand up my leg; it is cool from her beer. "I never thought I'd end up with him though. I thought it would be just a short term thing, but it lasted eight years." Rubia sips her beer. "We've been separated since February. I even called a lawyer last week, to make an appointment to try and finish it up."

"When did you know that we'd end up here, Rubia?"

She sifts her fingers through her hair, covers her face. " I don't know, Billy. It just worked out that way." But Rubia is lying. She knows the moment – on her couch when she cried. She knew then, like I knew when I saw her hair.

"Uh huh." I run my hands under her hair, lifting it up over our heads. I let it fall down among us in tangled waves.

"Come up here," I say, and Rubia does. And I kick the

White Dog

closet door shut with my foot.

Tonight we are at the Lighthouse, a country western bar right off the base in Norfolk. Chief Kenney and I sit at the wrap-around bar, and people dance the two-step in starched gingham and lace dresses, new blue jeans and black cowboy hats.

Chief Kenney looks out at the dance floor and smokes. He doesn't like being here. He has a wife and kid; he would like to be home with them. But he came here from a sense of duty. He had been the one that had told me my father died – now almost a month ago. So he feels that he needs to tell me that what I did with Rubia was wrong, that you don't sleep with widows – that is unacceptable. And he is smart enough and has seen enough to know exactly what I did; he has worked this job for six years and has seen officers come and go, every twenty-four months rotating off and on the ships. Some, I'm sure, he thinks were very professional. But I'm a trial to him.

Chief Kenney smokes each of his cigarettes down to the filter before he lights another one. His thumb is too fat for the child safety lock on the lighter; and so he stretches out each cigarette as long as it will go, afraid that the lighter will beat him eventually and leave him with nothing else to do but talk to me.

"How old was your Dad?" Chief Kenney finally says. He motions for two beers.

We get White Sheets from the Red Cross on the deceased, and they are filled with facts, like Date of Birth and Time of Death, so I know Chief Kenney has already read that my Pa was fifty-two. This is one of the reasons my Pa's death is hard for us. In our job, we rely on little tricks that only we are aware of, like the White Sheets, and we have our own language, with words like honors ceremony, death benefits, next of kin. Everything remains professional, as a job we are paid to do – Chief Kenney or I do the notification, arrange the funeral; one of us sits with the family to present the flag to the widow or mother at the proper moment.

Doug Frelke

By these methods, we make them believe we understand what they feel.

"Fifty-two," I say.

"That's young."

I nod. "Yep." Our beers arrive. I motion the bartender for a shot to go with mine. Chief looks away quickly, but I can see from the glance that he is nervous. He is thinking, 'now on top of everything else, the Lieutenant will drink too much.'

"It's hard," he says.

I laugh at that, too loud. I can feel a rising angry meanness. "You ever lose anyone close to you, Chief?"

Chief Kenney stubs his cigarette out. "No, sir. I've been lucky, I guess. My mother and father live out in Arkansas. They're healthy. My dad's eighty and my mom's seventy-four."

"So you've been lucky," I say.

"Mostly." Chief looks down the bar, away from me. Then he says, "I lost my dog when I was a kid. I had a dog named Boxer and we had to put him to sleep."

"That's a damn nice way to say you killed him, Chief."

Chief Kenney does not look at me; he looks pat my head back towards the restrooms and the cigarette machine.

"Anyway. You put him to sleep."

"Yeah. My dad got a new job and the job was in the city. You couldn't have dogs there. My mom said we would give him away, but I was old enough to know what would happen. My dad never liked dogs, never liked the country. That was why he got a job in the city."

"What did you do?"

Chief laughs. "I ran away with the dog and hid out in my Uncle's tobacco barn, about three miles away. I figured I could sleep there and live off the money from my paper route. I was eleven. I thought I had the whole thing worked out."

"What did your dad do?"

"My uncle called him and he came down. I remember my uncle saying to him when they walked into the barn,

White Dog

"Jess, you promised you wouldn't take it out on the boy." And my dad kept his word; he never touched me. He just dragged the dog off in his truck and I never saw him again."

"What happened after that?"

"Nothing. We moved to the city. I never got another dog."

"You could get one now for your kids."

Chief shrugged. "Yeah, I guess I could. But I won't, you know?"

"Yeah." I drink my beer and look away from the chief; give him time to work the lighter on another cigarette. "My Pa used to tell me stories. He was great with stories." I drop my shot into the bottom of my beer, raise the glass.

"I'll tell you one," I say.

He nods. "All right."

"This story's about Blackbeard's trick." I take a long drink, lick the foam from my lip to taste the sharpness of the whiskey. "I'll try to tell it like he would." The chief shakes his head, fine, and ashes fall from his cigarette, making gray streaks on his white blouse.

"Blackbeard was a pirate. He lived in Bath, North Carolina – he had a house there and a wife, and he spent his gold in the bars and taverns of the coastal towns. In return, the inn keepers and bar maids kept him informed; in this way, he knew when an English man-o-war was sent out of Norfolk to attempt to capture him.

"Blackbeard had a trick, though. He painted all the decks and bulkheads of his ship black, and he greased the ladders of his ship with lard. Then he would smear his own face with pitch and braid cords of black powder into the long strands of his hair and beard. Blackbeard would allow the English to spot him at twilight and they would chase him in and out of the coastal islands, until the sun had set and it was dark. Then, Blackbeard would find a cove and come about, letting his sails luff and dropping anchor. And he'd light his fuses, waiting."

Chief draws a cigarette from the pack, but he doesn't

17

Doug Frelke

light it; he just rolls it between his fingers as a comfort.

"The English Captain moored at the opposite side of the cove and sent his gig over, cautious of a trap. His sailors rowed across the cove, in the dark, to the very side of Blackbeard's ship; there, they climbed aboard to the upper deck, to shield them from an ambush. But there was no ambush – not even a crew. There was only Blackbeard, standing down on the middle of the main deck. And the only light came from the burning braids of his hair, haloing his face. Blackbeard paced the main deck and taunted the English sailors, banging his cutlass against the mast.

"One sailor rushed down in answer. His boot slid on the thick lard coating the ladder, and he fell to the lower deck. Blackbeard was already perfectly placed. He cut off the sailor's head on the first stroke. Then he picked that English head up by its hair, and strode across the deck to the main mast. He hung it there, on a ten-penny nail.

"Blackbeard's action brought the English down in angry screaming leaps. But they never reached him – either they slipped down to him, or they were killed by the other members of his crew, who had hidden in barrels or behind coils of rope. Until finally, just one, a coward, was left standing on the upper deck.

" 'Go home', Blackbeard said. And the English coward did. He jumped over the side to his gig and rowed, until he safely returned to the deck of the British man-o-war. There he told them what he had seen of Blackbeard – his black decks, his six foot tall frame, his face on fire, and the English head nailed to his mast.

" 'He is just a man', the English Captain told the coward. But the coward said, 'No, sir. He is the devil himself.'

"The Captain argued with reason, then he tried threats. Then he whipped the coward, to make him admit he was wrong. Eventually, the coward recanted. But the crew still believed the coward. And they refused to fight Blackbeard until their own officers pulled their pistols and forced them back across."

Chief places the cigarette in his mouth, lights it. He

White Dog

blows out hard, stiff white lines of smoke. "That's a good story."

"Yeah. I loved that story." I lift my beer, but my hand shakes and so I put it down quick. It tastes sour now, and I will not finish it.

"There's a little more though; something my Pa never told me. When I was in college, I looked Blackbeard up at the library, just to horse around. What I found out was the English did capture him eventually. And they nailed his own head to a fake mast outside the courthouse, while his surviving pirates were tried and hanged."

Chief nods. "That's what happens to pirates."

"Yeah. But don't you think my Pa should have told me that part?"

Chief finishes his beer. "No. I don't think so." He shrugs. "It was his story."

I put twenty dollars on the table as a kind of insult – the griever paying for the consoler. "Well, I guess it's my story now," I say, sliding out from behind the bar. "See you tomorrow, Chief."

Chief lifts his hand. "Yes, sir."

I turn back. "Do you hate your uncle, chief, for turning you in?"

Chief blinks. He nods. "Yeah. I never thought about it much, but I can't stomach the man."

I nod. "See, that's convenient – you have one person to hate and one to love. Mine's all mixed up. I still hate my Pa for leaving me and it's stupid because now he's dead. What do you do about that, Chief?"

The chief looks at my face, his eyes to mine. "I don't know, sir. That's a hell of a thing."

I nod – nothing to say. And I work my way over to the door and out, into the brightness of the street.

After Rubia, Chief Kenney gave me a break for awhile from the visits. I stuck with the phone work – calling the hospital morgue, arranging the funeral, staffing the honor guard from local detachments. Chief would go out by himself for the notifications. I stayed in the office for three

Doug Frelke

weeks.

I don't know exactly what made me decide I wanted to go out again. I drove into work like usual and it was a cool spring day, brighter than warm and the sky was that unreal spring blue with white clouds moving across, like a thin herd of animals. A good day for a drive, I thought, and so I told Chief I was taking the one that came across the fax that morning, on John James.

John James's parents were in Bath, North Carolina, out towards the water and New Bern, where my Pa is buried. I lied to the chief and told him I wanted to stop off to see my Pa's grave – that seemed to calm him. But I hadn't even read the rest of the White Sheet, and so I didn't learn that John James's death had been a suicide until I was deep into Blackbeard's country.

I pulled over to the side of the road and read John James's story as trucks shook past me and family station wagons headed to their river houses. He had been just a kid, barely twenty-one, a good sailor, up for promotion to petty officer. His carrier, the Roosevelt, had been steaming off the California coast, coming home to San Diego and making good time in clear seas. Sometime between midnight and four A.M., on the fifth of April, John James had stepped off his ship into the Pacific Ocean.

He had been the aft lookout; when the watch switched, his relief found John's clothes piled next to the safety rail. The whole set-up was like a good trick, only one where you've looked away at the exact wrong moment and missed the magic.

The relief found John James's clothes: neatly folded dungarees and his white T-shirt, his boots laced together and tied to the post, his wallet and belt slid into the toes of his boots to keep the wind from blowing them over the side. The politeness of this final image nails me: John James, tall and naked on the edge of the deck, bending to patiently tie his boots to the rail.

It takes me an hour from the highway to find his parents' place, having to double back when the roads go to dirt and gravel. Out here, the road names are written on

White Dog

wood slats, with names like, "Old Hook Road" and "Kaylen's Way," and they are often overgrown by brush or obscured by peeling paint, so you have to stop the car to read them. I get to the James's just before noon; a cinder block ranch, with thick white paint layered on the concrete and a worn redwood deck that circles the whole house, like a faded ring.

A white dog sleeps under the deck. I hesitate for a second, waiting for the dog to bark and for the people to come out and grab hold of him. But the white dog doesn't bark. He just lies there in the shade of the deck – a bird dog, with blue eyes and a long thin noble nose.

A tall man comes out of the house. He picks up a shotgun from the edge of the stoop. He checks the sight. Then he levels it at me, moving his finger to the trigger.

The dog barks, and a woman yells from inside the door. John's mother, Idalia James, steps out onto deck. Nearly six-foot, she wears a pair of men's overalls over a pink T-shirt. She grabs the gun from her husband, Jonah, and he ages suddenly, standing there beside her.

Idalia James calls over to the car. "You can come out, Mister." She has a high voice, a choir singer.

"I'm okay," I say.

"We already know, Mister." She breaks the gun, removes the shells. "I figured the Navy would send someone. I've been keeping an eye on Jonah all day, but I guess he got away from me."

I sit in the car – unable to say anything else, unable to move.

Idalia cups her hand over her eyes, looks towards the car. "Mister, you can come in if you like."

Idalia James comes down the drive to fetch me. She takes me by the shoulder, with big hands that are oversized for a woman and strong. Still, they are ladylike, with long clean fingers and nails painted pink in a shade that matches her T-shirt. I move some, then, but it is like she is lifting me from the car with those hands. "Why don't you come round the back. Jonah will make you some lemonade."

Doug Frelke

Idalia leads me to the rear of the house where the backyard falls off into the water of the Pamlico Sound and bits of old wood and trash bob in the edge of the grass. She helps me to a green plastic chair that faces the water, and sits down beside me. Jonah shuffles out of the back of the house with a pitcher of lemonade.

Idalia pours and Jonah mixes the drinks, adding shots of gin. He makes the first one – lifts the glass, wipes the sides clean. Then he passes it to me, the guest. Such politeness. And I can't help but to see his son again, on the edge of his ship's deck.

I take a sip and the lemonade is hard and cool, the gin catching in my throat. "I'm sorry about your son." I look at them, and their faces crack along the worn fault-lines of their recent grief – chapped lips shiver, eyes blinking too fast.

Jonah speaks, "His birthday's next month. He'd be twenty-one, then."

"That's young," I say.

"How old are you, Mister?" Idalia asks. She doesn't look at me; she watches her fingers trace thick lines in the cloth. Jonah pulls his eyes from the water, back to me.

"I'm twenty-four."

Jonah raises his voice, his face flushing with the gin. "Then you should know. Why does a boy like that kill himself? Why does he do a thing like that? That's what I want someone to drive out here and tell me."

A minute passes, then another and I cannot think of what to say. Jonah is steeled for an answer; Idalia runs her hand over the tablecloth, cleaning it with the palm of her hand.

"My Pa died two months ago," I say.

No more words are spoken. Jonah drains his lemonade, pours another. Then, Idalia stretches across the little table; she puts her big hands on either side of my face, as if she is trying to hold it together for me. And I begin to cry.

"It's hard," she says.

We sit together and drink, looking out at the water. Idalia passes me a tissue, and I wipe my face. Jonah talks

White Dog

about the weather – how good the rain has been for the corn. Idalia talks about the white dog. "A white dog around here. That's a sign. It's a suicide ghost. That's how we knew." Her voice mixes with the easy slaps of the water – the same voice she used to get me out of the car – same solidness.

The dog came down the road one evening. They couldn't get it to eat, it wouldn't come out from under the porch. And so they believed it was the ghost of their son, coming back home to say good bye to them. And I think that is a strange thing to believe, but then I think of the dog under the porch and how he barked at just the right time and then Idalia came outside. And yet no dog followed us around the back, no sign of a dog anywhere now.

Jonah says, "Mister, what was your Pa's name? Was he from around here?"

"He was. He went away for a while. Then he came back." I squint out at the sun, grown huge in the midday sky. "His name was Billy Ray. Same as mine."

Jonah scratches his head; he does not know of my father, but he doesn't want to say that. Idalia refills my glass and Jonah mixes in the gin.

Idalia asks, "What do you remember about your Pa?"

Out on the water, the sunlight reflects stunning rows of brightness; there are so many scenes, so many remembrances flooding into my head. But I only voice the first few, feeble and weak. "I remember my mom said that when they were kids everyone thought he looked like Elvis, but he couldn't sing at all. He liked to drink gin and tonics, and used to mix them up in the biggest glass he could find in the house, an old brandy snifter." I realize that what I am saying does not make any real sense to the James' – I am too new at this. My thoughts are not organized, not put together well. I need more practice. "He was a natural born story teller – he used to tell stories all the time."

Jonah leans back in his chair. "John never wore his glasses. I had to drive to Raleigh to get him these special glasses. He hated them. So he never wore them, just got

Doug Frelke

used to squinting."

Idalia smiles. "John had his own will but he wasn't willful, you know? He wrote us cards, real personal ones about how much we meant to him – birthday, Father's Day, every holiday."

Jonah swallows his lemonade. "You could tell he worked hard on those cards."

Idalia pushes back from the table. "I still have every single one he ever gave me – back to when he was six." She shields her eyes. "It sure is a scorcher today, Billy," Idalia says, waving at the sun. "Why don't you stay for dinner?"

I stay past supper until late in the evening; I sit with them and look at pictures of John – as a baby, dressed as a hobo for Halloween, his high school prom, in his cracker-jacks from boot camp. Afterwards, they volunteer to drive me out to the main road. By then a mist has rolled in, and I can't see the road signs anymore. I stay close to their Chevrolet, with its one red taillight out in front of me and nothing at all off to the sides, just blackness and a harsh sea wind blowing in cold and wet through my window. When we get to the main road they honk and Jonah waves, his long arm sticking out and over the roof of their car like a flag. And I drive home.

I drive home through the swamps and low country and stratch pine, on unlit roads. My eyes are tired, but I still see them all – my Pa, Eddie Hayden, Frank Baxter, John James – one in the hint of a broken pine tree lining the road, one in a quick glance crossing through my side mirror, my Pa and BlackBeard taking turns riding in the seat next to mine. They are all there – heavy handed or faint ghost fingered – offering what they can in the way of comfort.

Push

"Watch this. Watch this boy cross the street." E.J. loves to watch the kid. And I have to admit I do, too, so I look up from the stack of pink carbon copies, November's bills of sale. E.J. points through the big glass showroom window, out over the new Cadillacs and the used red-neck Cameros and Firebirds, out across the street to the diner where Haint went to get himself a coke.

"You know that boy gets his cokes for free – Florida passes them to him all day long. Me, she lights into if I even try to get an extra coffee."

"I imagine he asks different," I say, but my boss isn't listening to me, he's watching, waiting for the kid to come back out of the diner. We wait quietly, a little nervous even, because with the kid you have a steady feeling that he could vanish just like that if you take your eye off him – no more walk, no more curly brown hair, no more white teeth all in his sharp row of a smile.

Haint comes out of Florida's with his fresh coke. He brushes a hand through his hair, using his fingers as a comb, then he waits for the traffic to pick up. Haint

Doug Frelke

won't start across the four lanes of Dickinson Avenue to E.J.'s car lot, Jefferson Motors, until he has an audience.

E.J. hitches up his raspberry slacks. "See. That fucking kid."

I watch. Haint steps into the road, so close on the heels of a red Trans-Am that his navy blazer brushes over the rear spoiler. Then he turns left and walks towards an oncoming car, a green Volvo with a blond lady behind the wheel. Haint keeps his pace. Two seconds before she would have screeched her brakes, Haint rolls right and fills the gap of the other lane. The Volvo skates past him; the blond woman too stunned to cuss him or even give him the finger.

And Haint stands patient on the median sipping his coke, waiting to finish the other half of the street as if he were painting a picture. Then, eight more steps, slow goddamn slow steps as if nothing could ever rush him, and he touches the macadam of our car lot.

"He's an artist," I say. E.J. nods; he knows what I mean for once. Still, he says, "I don't give two fucks about what that kid is. All I know is he's pure bred money and you don't mess with that."

Which is E.J.'s way of warning me to let it go. He's afraid I'll somehow mess up his great deal, by over thinking Haint. And I don't say anything to E.J., because he's dead right – that's how I messed up with Leonora over twenty years ago – when I had her and he didn't.

E.J. is as dumb as nails, but he knows me.

E.J. scratches his chin. He opens a new pouch of Levi Garrett, and the smell of molasses sifts through the pine sided office. E.J. pulls out a fair sized hunk and rolls a ball in the palm of his hand. He squeezes it into his right cheek. "You want some?"

"Yeah, throw it over here." I make myself a smaller chew, just a taste. I always feel self-conscious in the office – the whole place is glass, including the wall behind my desk. The glass is so the customers can look

Push

in and see the cars, but we're in here too, like an old cracked fishbowl. I know they can see us, catch me sneaking a drink or E.J. plucking his nose hairs out with his Swiss army tweezers. And we look out too, or at least I do, watching the mechanics' fist fights, kids getting smacked by mothers late to the grocery, young lovers paired and locked as they hurry past to walk-up apartments and fold out beds. All ordinary life – trash and junk. Twenty-five years.

E.J. turns from the window. "You think the kid is banging Florida?"

I shrug. I don't prefer to think like that – it makes me feel old, older than forty-seven, which is old as hell. But even though he just turned fifty, E.J. loves to talk like that, and he likes to bring up things we did when we were kids, when Leonora and I would double with him and his steady, a crazy girl from the Teacher's College, Eva, who was almost six-feet tall and said she was studying to be a drama instructor. He loves to talk about those times, but to me those stories are all dead now – whatever life was once in them has faded and is gone, like headlines from old newspapers.

But E.J. won't let it go. "I mean if I was ten years younger, I'd go after her. I'd say she's just touching her thirties – a nice looking black woman like that. I bet she's wild; I bet she could get right into you, a girl like that."

I wrinkle my face and E.J. laughs. "I'm just talking, Graham." I search around my desk for a Styrofoam coffee cup, so I can spit. "She's thirty-two," I say; though I'm guessing, I'm pretty sure I'm right. I'm normally pretty sure of most things, and maybe that's part of the reason I like the kid so much, because he's a black hole that just sucks up all my finest reasoning. Still, E.J. may be right about Haint and Florida. If so, good for the kid. Florida's black; or more directly half black, mixed with some Indian or Mexican blood, but here that doesn't make any real difference. She's just the same as straight black. Still, Florida has always taken care of her looks, with her nails painted and her hair straightened, and she carries herself like she knows she is something special – different, but special.

Florida is the type of woman E.J and I would have called an African queen, back when we were young and if he had been chasing her. But since Haint has been here, she's changed. She wears those African blouses with the dark greens and bright yellows, and her skirts are shorter. She ties her hair back behind her head with a gold ribbon now, instead of a white plastic clip.

"Hey." Haint walks in sipping his coke. "I sold that Barracuda for eighteen hundred bucks."

"I thought we were waiting on Johnson to fix the door on that one. The damn window on the passenger side won't roll down."

"Oh." Haint shrugs. He is already past the deal, forgetting it. "Didn't seem to matter much to the boy that bought it. He paid in cash." And Haint pulls out a roll of money, some of it bank fresh twenties, but most of it in grimy tens and fives, money from a high school kid, long saved and waiting.

"Sold as is." E.J. says, and spits into the tin waste bucket.

"No. You got to fix the window, E.J. That guy's going to come back here."

E.J. starts to say, "let the bastard come back," and I even hear him say it because that is one of his famous lines. But Haint nods to me and he says, "Right. We have to fix the window. He's bringing his brother in to look at a caddy."

The kid is pure genius. To a car salesman, luxury cars are total cream and dreaming – the high of ridiculous profit, a forty-percent mark up and a fat commission – steak dinners, home runs, salesman of the year. You do that once a month and it will get you through the lean times when you can't sell anything, when you are sure you've lost it and watch one deal after another fall through your fingers and your friends are afraid to talk to you because they can hear the desperation in

Push

your voice. With Haint here, we sell Caddies once a week and Lincolns and Mercedes, too. And most of the time it's Haint, but I've sold a few and so has E.J., and E.J.'s son, Reed, has even sold one. Though I think Haint pretty much pushed that one through for him.

    Sales is all thinking – thinking you can push a person to do what you want, what you need them to do. But how you execute the concept of the push is an exact and perfect thing.

    If you push too hard, they walk away; too soft, and the whole thing just stretches out forever, like melting taffy. The push has to be just right, and Haint can push, dollar for dollar, better than anyone I've ever seen. We all watch him – even E.J. is picking up some little stuff, using one of Haint's lines, "So, how are you feeling today?" Haint says it like he has sugar in his mouth and it doesn't matter how you felt before he asked because now you feel so goddamn good.

    Haint will say, "You feeling like driving a new car?" Or "You feeling like spending some money?" But those lines don't sound right just hearing them, and the words don't matter anyway. It's Haint's delivery, what he is saying with the words. Because what he is really saying is do you feel like exchanging that old thing you called a life for this new thing that I can give you, that I can rock you into like a lullaby, give it to you with a little piece of me which is what I'm really selling and what you are really buying – a time share piece of the Haint experience. Me, I don't touch any of his lines. I don't have what he has, and I know it. But now we'll fix that fucking window on the Barracuda, and Haint will probably sell the brother, too.

    Haint salutes us and we salute back. I don't know why we started the salutes; its just a dumb thing we've started to do, something Haint came up with when Reed sold an old Catalina and now it's stuck. We salute all the time now, every deal; it's become part of the sale. Haint takes his coke and walks back out into the sun.

    E.J. sticks his head out of the double glass doors of

Doug Frelke

the entrance way and spits into the planter of weeds behind them that used to be begonias. "You know my daughter, China Lee?"

I nod. I've known China Lee since she was born. She's E.J.'s baby doll. She's close to sixteen now, and she works here on Saturdays, typing invoices and filing, but mainly she does what the rest of us do, she watches Haint. And her daddy sent her home last week for wearing some MTV outfit – a half cut halter sweater and a skirt that didn't cover the whole of her butt.

"Well, I had Haint over to dinner last month because he'd won the salesman of the quarter award, right?"

I smile. Haint was the very first award winner to ever receive that honor – it smacked of China Lee. The normal "winners" were either me or E.J., but we gave it to Reed once when he sold two cars in a week.

"Graham, I think my daughter China Lee is after Haint."

This is a well-known thing around the lot; like usual, E.J. is the last to notice. I noticed a few weeks ago, knew for sure when Leonora started stopping by the lot with China Lee. That is something Leonora almost never does – she knows it pains me to see her. But now with the kid here, I'm sure China Lee is all over her to stop in whenever possible and they drop off lunch for Reed or pick him up to ride down to Parker's Restaurant.

"I can understand China Lee. She's too much like me to fool me. But I can't figure Leonora in this. She's more complicated. Why do you think she's helping China Lee?"

"My guess is she's just looking for something to do, maybe a kind of challenge." I spit into the cup, swirling the thick brown stain up the sides, letting it drip back down. "But that's just a guess, E.J. You give me too much credit for knowing Leonora's mind."

E.J. laughs. "That fucking kid. I hope he can handle it all." He moves the wad of tobacco from one side of

Push

his mouth to the other. "But I'm okay with it. Haint's the best damn salesman I ever had."

"Yeah." E.J. loves the money Haint brings in and China Lee isn't too high of a price to pay. But Leonora is much harder to figure; she has always hated the cars and the lot and the salesmen. I even see it in the way she treats her own son, Reed, now that he is down here full time. To Leonora, we are all on the con, oily tricksters and rip-off artists. But she doesn't seem to hold anything against Haint.

I look over my papers. "Aw, hell. I stained my tally sheet with your tobacco. I was adding up November's commissions so I could post the winner." The salesman of the month award was worth five hundred dollars, and I always took it serious.

E.J. shakes his head. "It doesn't matter, Graham. Out of the four of us, is anyone close to Haint?"

I check the final line of figures. "You and me have around five thousand this month." Though I had E.J. beat by about three hundred dollars. "Reed has a little over three. He sold that Cadillac and two Oldsmobiles."

"And Haint?" E.J. spits into the old Mack cylinder I used as an ashtray.

"Hey, don't spit in that. It's an ashtray." I hand him another Styrofoam cup. "Here." E.J. took the cup and spit again, just to spit. "He has around ten thousand, give or take a couple hundred."

"Shit. That boy's a gold mine. November's his fifth straight month."

"Yeah, I know. That's why I wanted to tally the figures in case anyone asked."

"Like who?"

I move my head to the cup and spit. "I don't know. Reed maybe."

E.J. sucks in his mouth, and the wad of tobacco stands out like a golf ball in his cheek. "Haint is a goddamn lucky star. I mean I love the kid, you love the kid, hell, Reed even likes him and Reed doesn't like anyone. You've got to relax some, Graham. Live a little.

Doug Frelke

This time is the tit's ass for us. Lean in and squeeze a little."

"Sure." But I can't. How can a thing like this last? And so I count and tally all the numbers, so I will have proof before Haint fades into more of E.J.'s stories. I have worked beside E.J. since I came back from my stint in the Navy almost twenty-five years ago. He isn't a half bad closer when there's a little competition, but it's been a long while since my heart was in it enough to be competitive. We've each sold more cars in six months with Haint than we sold all of last year, hell almost all of the last two years.

E.J. is right though, I should lean into it, because right now I am at the top of my own game, never mind Haint. I sold two Cadillacs this month; one to a stock broker who bought out all the options: power everything, a cellular, four way Alpine speakers with a custom CD changer in the trunk. I am a giant now – huge, brimming full. I haven't lived like this since I was eighteen and thought I was going to marry Leonora and have my best friend, Elijah James, go into business with me. And I can't lean into the Haint experience because I don't want to get hooked into that feeling again. It'll make it too hard when I have to go back to being small again.

Stories. History. What we have to pass off as memories never seem to stay put – we bend them, forget the main parts, break them up and crush the juice out of them. Even with Haint. The story of how I hired Haint is getting worn now. We have told it so many times that we have begun to tell the customers. When a story gets so old that it becomes a sales story, it is time to kill it and put it out of its misery. But I can't do that with Haint's story. I can't box it up and stow it away.

I remember Haint came in at the beginning of summer, because spring was just over and that is always a rough time for me – somehow spring is what gets me through the rest of the year and when it passes I

Push

am always unsure of what to link onto for a couple of weeks. That was how I was feeling when Haint came in looking for a job.

Haint walked into my office around ten. The day was already in the eighties and it had rained during the night, so everything was wet and sticky and uncomfortable. Haint looked cool, though. And it wasn't just a matter of not sweating – Haint had never thought to sweat. He possessed a high running cool, like it was his natural temperature, and the first thing he told me when I interviewed him was that he was an artist.

"Like with paint?"

"Mainly. Sometimes charcoal. I tried clay, but I didn't like the feel."

I nodded, turning his resume over on my desk. "Well, thanks for coming in. We're really looking for a man with experience."

"Sure." And that was when I felt the first whoosh of his cool; he lifted his face to me and I saw those small hairs on his chin that made it seem like he was still too young to even have to shave yet. Whoosh.

Haint said, "What do you get if that lady over there buys one of those fancy Cadillacs? What kind of commission does a sales representative make on a deal like that?"

I shrugged. "You sell that car you make five-percent, plus a bonus since we've been carrying that car close to ninety days on our floorplan. The bonus would be another two point five percent for getting it off our loan." I worked my adding machine. "Sticker price is thirty-four thousand, three hundred and two dollars. So if you sold it at sticker, which never happens anymore, you would receive a sales commission of two thousand five hundred seventy-two dollars and sixty-five cents. After taxes, you'd pocket around seventeen hundred dollars."

Haint whistled. "That's good money. You could make a fine living selling cars."

I shook my head. "Sure, kid, you could. Or you

33

Doug Frelke

could starve. I have salesmen working on debit, which means they owe me when and if they ever sell another car." I ran my hand towards the show room. "That lady you think you could sell? She's a widow. She comes in once a week, every week. She asks questions. Sometimes she takes a test drive, if it's a nice day. She drives a seventy-eight Lincoln her husband left her." I brushed my hand against my forehead, to shake off the layer of sweat. "That's all she'll ever drive, son."

The kid moved his lips, counting in his head.

"Look, I got other people to see."

"Sure. I know. But see, I already sold her the car."

I pushed my chair back, and buzzed the desk to send in China Lee. "So what did she offer?"

"What it said on the sticker. But I told her I could get her a set of floor mats for free."

I laughed. "Boy, that's something. You are an artist." I smacked the blotter on my desk. "But why don't you get yourself enrolled out at the college and teach something, instead of wasting a busy man's time?"

China Lee stuck her head in. "Yeah, Graham?"

"Could you show this boy out? Give him a coke on me, all right?"

The kid rose, and offered his hand, slick and patient. China Lee looked at the kid. "Haint, that lady buying the Cadillac wants to know if she can get a pair of black mats instead of blue. She thinks the black will wear better."

"Yeah, I think that's fine. Is that fine, Mr. Graham?"

I was standing by my chair, still shaking the kid's hand, with its perfect coolness.

"Fuck," I said.

China Lee wrinkled her nose. "You shouldn't cuss, Graham. You know my Daddy hates that. Plus, Haint's new here and I'm trying to make a good impression for Jefferson Motors."

"Sure." I said. "I apologize." But I was watching the widow in the showroom. She was running her hand

Push

over the car, her new car, petting it like it was this great big thirty-four-thousand dollar dog Haint had just given her to keep her company. "China Lee, give him Bobby's desk. I don't think he's ever coming back, since he owes us three grand. And the name's just Graham, son. No mister."

"Yes, sir. I'm Joshua Haint."

"You can start on Monday if you like, Haint."

"I'd like to start now, if it's fine."

"Sure, sure. That's fine. Close the door on your way out, China Lee."

She took Haint's hand and closed the door behind her. "That fucking kid," I said. Then I opened the bottom drawer, the one that sticks when its hot. I pulled out the flask of scotch I keep under my high school year book, Lincoindale, 1966. I drank a long cool sip, and a laugh came to my throat, like a bubble, like after watching a ninth inning homerun or hitting a hundred dollar ticket, only more crazy and wild and cool.

Leonora drives a white Mercedes with red leather interior; E.J. buys her the new model every January. Of course he gets a deal, but he's still got to go down to Wilson and make the order and the Mercedes guy there sticks him a little, just because the Mercedes guy knows that we would stick him if he was trying to buy a Cadillac – that's just what you have to put up with in this business. So I see the car, know it's Leonora. She comes in, wearing big cat's eye sun glasses.

"Graham, have you seen Haint?"

"He's working, Leonora."

She lowers her glasses down her nose. She has her hair pulled back in a bright green scarf; I can't help but think that she is something, some kind of special thing, standing there with her long black hair and the glasses and the green scarf. "I know, Graham," she says. "Could you tell him I stopped by?"

"Sure, Leonora." She shakes her head, turns to go. I wait until she has the door in her hand; then I say,

35

Doug Frelke

"Could I tell him what it's about?"

She stops. Leonora raises her fist to her face, covers her mouth. It is an old gesture of hers – she is thinking about something else, not really listening to me, using her fist to cover her thoughts. "Just tell him I need to talk to him about China Lee."

"Okay," I say. Leonora places her glasses back on her face as if she were righting a picture along the wall; then she steps out of the office. I watch her walk the lot to her Mercedes. Her heels stumble on the uneven gravel. She shoots glances out through the car rows, and I can tell she is getting old then, too near sighted to see Haint on the far side of the lot, among the cheaper cars, the trade-ins and the wrecks. Leonora slides behind the red leather wheel and folds down the visor to check herself in the vanity; she pats her cheeks hard to flush the color. Then she starts the Mercedes – in one turn, the car is alive and the engine is full-throttle – ready to respond to her, take her where she wants to go. She shifts out of park and moves slowly, with last looks in her mirror, out to the left and right, over her shoulder. She hits Dickinson Avenue, signals, merges with the traffic. Then she is gone.

Haint is working an old black woman on the far corner of the lot. Her white pill-box hat glints and shines in the rising sun, nodding and flashing as she talks to Haint. They are in front of a faded red Pacer. "Why's he wasting his time on that piece of junk?" E.J. says.

"I asked him to. We almost own that car outright and we need to get it off the floor plan." E.J. likes to sell the luxury cars, the Lincolns and Cadillacs, or the high priced foreign trade-ins, the BMW's and Mercedes. But I do all the paperwork so I know the lot's loan amount, the floor plan, and you have to move all the cars to keep from getting hit by the bank. "You don't want to buy the cars, you want the customers to buy the cars." That is another of E.J. lines, but he

Push

doesn't live by it. So I normally get stuck working the piece of shit trade-ins, the small bitter deals, where cash payment is required, and there are no test drives unless you have something to show me. And I don't like it either, so I pawn the cars off as quick as I can to the blacks or migrant workers or some white trash teenager who wants to sign over his McDonald's checks for his first car.

"Well, son of a bitch. That's got to be a new record." E.J. spits his chew into the wastebasket. He pulls out his pocket mirror and checks his hair; wipes the tobacco juice from his lips, smooths his eyebrows. When he is pretty enough, he scoots down to his office to get the keys to the Pacer off of the wafer-board behind his desk.

Haint is coming over with the customer, taking his own time. His hand cups the old woman's elbow, helping her along. He nods and smiles while she talks, probably about her grandkids, or her church. I know Haint is enjoying himself, which is fair. The close of a sale is a sweet little jewel, like when you were a kid tricking the juice out of a honeysuckle. You want to stretch out your tongue and roll in the taste. Even in a little shit deal.

I go over the paperwork – we have about four fifty in the car, between the initial trade and some minor work we had to get done with the lights. We have it listed at twelve hundred; knowing Haint he will probably bring her in high, too, maybe even a full grand. So we double our money. That's the thing E.J. misses about these deals.

There's solid money in the used market, if you can move them. Everybody needs a car and lots of real people are never going to be able to slide their asses behind the wheel of a Lincoln or a Cadillac. Most of the world drives Pacers and Catalinas or Hondas, Tercels, Buicks, Fords – the average non-luxury, boring automobile. Nine hundred would be mighty fine too, if that's all he could get.

Doug Frelke

Haint helps the old lady up the steps and E.J. runs over to open the screen door. Haint brings her over to the chair across from E.J.'s desk. I get up and stand in the doorway, just to watch.

"This is Mrs. Green. She has an interest in that Pacer out there."

E.J. works his head up and down the lot, then winces. "My Pacer? Boy, that sure is a nice looking car. I was sort of keeping an eye on it for myself. My daughter's just shy of sixteen and I thought that one would be perfect for her." When E.J. lies, he smiles and smiles – that is how you can tell. He only bothers to hold that wide friendly smile of his when he needs it. "You have any children, Mrs. Green?"

Mrs. Green sits upright in the chair, a slight woman, her blue leather pocketbook balanced on her knees. She wears a blue dress and white gloves with her white silk pill-box hat – dressed for a special occasion, like going to church or buying a new car. "I sure do. Three children and five grandchildren." Mrs. Green relaxes a bit against the back of the chair. She looks over to Haint and smiles at him, flashing her two golden front teeth. The rest of her teeth are raggle-edged and split, yellowed. But those two gold teeth shine prettily against her black lips, and she seems to move her mouth to accentuate them and hide the rest, as if they were recent additions she is especially proud of. "Only one of the girls live around here. The rest moved West or North."

E.J. nods in sympathy. "Yeah, it's getting tough to keep the young ones around with all the New York styles and such. I've got two myself, a boy and a girl. The boy works here with me. But all my daughter ever talks about is going to New York City or California."

"Well, I've got my baby here, and she takes care of me; drives me to the services at the church and keeps me from getting lonely. But even she's thinking of leaving now. That's why I'm looking for a car." There is a flicker of fear in Mrs. Green's eyes, a fish tail twirling in a still pond. Then her brown eyes smooth, and she is cheerful again.

"What you need, Mr. Phillips, is a few more children. Young man like you could always have a few more." Mrs. Green emphasizes her gold teeth. I look over at Haint – Mrs. Green is working E.J. a little.

E.J raises his hands off the desk, as if in surrender. "Well, Mrs. Green I'm a bit older than I look for that. Besides, I definitely think my wife is through with the babies." E.J. pats his hair. "So what are you offering for that Pacer?"

Haint had positioned himself behind Mrs. Green, and now he lets his left hand rest on her shoulder. "I told Mrs. Green I'd see what I could do for her. I was thinking six-fifty would be fair."

E.J.'s smile never leaves his face. His hands are shoved under the desk out of sight, where he can crack his knuckles and fidget with the without alerting the customer. But I know him and I can tell he is pissed, trying to figure Haint. Because it seems like such a failure. Anyone, even Reed, could have moved the car for eight hundred.

E.J. purses his lips like he was spitting again. "Haint, if that's what you think is fair," but E.J. doesn't even look at him, "then you and Graham fill out the title. I have to go see to one of the other customers." There is no one out on the lot – we can all see that through the glass, but Mrs. Green and I nod along. Haint doesn't do a damn thing, just keeps his eyes on E.J.

E.J. takes Mrs. Green's hand. "Nice doing business with you, Mrs. Green. I'm sure you'll enjoy that Pacer." He leaves the office like a bullet then and the glass doors to the outside swing and bang until they work themselves closed.

I take the keys from E.J.'s desk and show Mrs. Green where to sign. I write her out a receipt and fill out the bill of sale, placing the pink copy in my pile and writing HAINT along the right-hand corner. I thank her, shake her hand, and then she is gone. She walks off the lot with her pill-box hat firm against her head and her

Doug Frelke

little blue pocketbook that holds the keys to her new car wedged tightly against her hip. Haint waves as she pulls off.

Haint moves around the lot, slow, taking his time. He knows I am waiting for him, waiting to talk to him.

"What the hell is up with you, Haint? Anyone could have gotten eight hundred for that car."

"That's Florida's mom, Graham. Did you know that?"

"No. I didn't." But I relax some, since that makes sense, even more so if E.J. was right about Florida and Haint. When I tell E.J he will understand that, maybe even enjoy it.

"I'll pay the difference between the six-fifty and the eight hundred out of my pocket. Plus I owe you another fifty or so because I had Montee put in new sparks and change the oil."

"Shit, Haint. Don't tell E.J. that part." I move the papers around my desk, throw out my chew and the spit cup. "Where's Florida going?"

"Out West. She says she can't stay here any longer."

"Yeah. I can understand that. You think she can make it out West in that piece of shit?"

Haint smiles, his eyes narrowing in the effort. "I sure as hell hope so."

The next day E.J. got a call from Leonora and China Lee. They were down at the beach house, using the early part of the week to get the place ready for Thanksgiving. The women had taken a Suburban down there, filled to the windows with groceries and pans and small appliances until it had just managed to limp into the beach house driveway with two flat tires. E.J. asked if I'd go down and there and change the tires. I'd been there a few times for his birthday and Leonora's parties, so I knew where it was.

Haint was outside, roaming the lot when E.J. got the call; but he must have heard the story through our mechanic, Montee. Haint had Montee put our hydraulic jack in the trunk of a Mercedes sportster we had on consignment from E.J.'s dentist's wife. When I went around to the garage, Haint was in the Mercedes – top down, ready to go, looking comfortable in the driver's seat.

"You know where this place is?" Haint clicks the steering wheel back and forth, like he is already driving.

"Yeah. I know where it is. E.J. said you can go, too?"

"I didn't ask E.J." Haint stands up in the car, leaning over the windshield. "Hey, Montee. You tell the boss I rode up with Graham to help with the tires."

Montee looks at me, but his black eyes settle on Haint.

"Sure. I'll tell him, Haint."

"Great. Let's go, Graham. Let's head to the beach." Haint slaps his hands against the leather of the passenger seat. "Get in."

"You have any gas?"

"Sure. Plenty. Let's go." Haint begins to race the engine shaking the fiberglass sides of the garage. "Come on, Graham."

So I get in. "You need gas, Haint. The needle is on empty."

"We are all right, Mr. Graham. Lay back and rest easy. We are all right."

"It's forty miles, Haint."

Haint laughs, shooting out past our pumps, not even slowing, never considering. "Look at this day, Graham, look at this goddamn day." And I did look at the day, but I also said that if we ran out of gas he was walking to fetch the tank.

But I had to admit the cocky bastard was right; the day was bright and the moon was still in the sky, so you had the moon and the sun above you and you felt sure that even the moon was giving off some warmth, like on a special deal delivered just for you. Haint put the heat to the floor for our feet, but it was warm anyway,

Doug Frelke

with the sun on our faces. Driving in the bright winter sunlight – so much softer than the heavy southern summer heat, all light and shine – and you just breath in the rushing air, lean your head out and dip right into the stream of it, let the day grab hold of you. We took the back roads, and on a weekday morning in November no one was heading to the beach, so we drove on empty roads for miles until we'd come upon a tractor or an old sedan making thirty miles an hour. Then Haint would signal using his hands, old fashioned and comic, and slide over without checking the lane. We'd pass them at eighty miles an hour. "Wave," Haint would say and I would, to some old farmer working his fields or a farmer's wife heading for groceries at the Piggly-Wiggly. We drove just shy of an hour like that, straight through to Leonora's house.

At the beach house, we pull into the driveway and park under the faded mint green house, between the grey hurricane stilts. The Suburban is on the other side of the gravel and the left side is down, front and back.

"China Lee probably hit a curb," I say.

"Yeah." Haint climbs out of the car without opening the door.

He walks toward the water, following the boardwalk towards the beach until he gets to the top of the dunes. A good wind is coming over, blowing sand that stings the side of my face as I get out. "What are you looking at, Haint?"

He points, his eyes screwed down from the sand and the wind. "Those two."

Down past the dunes, two women run in and out of the surf, kicking foam and splashing. The tide is rough with the wind and the beach is covered with a spread of brown-white sea foam. The women bend down and gather handfuls of the foam, tossing it in the air. The wind grabs it, carrying some of the foam up over the dunes, while the rest falls to the sand in clumps, scattering as it hits the ground like fast little crabs. It takes me a full minute before I recognize the women as Leonora

Push

and China Lee.

"I'm going to put the top up on the Mercedes, Haint. Before the car fills with sand."

"Okay. You do that, Graham." Haint runs down the dune, behind the women. They don't see him until he has already joined in, grabbing great gobs of foam in both hands and throwing it at them. They turn and chase him. I hear their screams and laughs; I know Leonora's throaty one – China Lee's is higher pitched, but much like her mother's. Haint's is the loudest, cutting through wind. He screams and shouts as he runs from them, throwing his jacket to slow them, trying to climb up the dunes on all fours. I watch as they catch him, Leonora with one arm and China Lee locking up the other. They start to drag him down the dune and then he breaks into another run, a full gallop, but they are still holding tight to his arms until he is pulling them, full tilt into the water. They crash out into the water, splashing, until all three of them are standing in the surf up to their knees.

I go down to the car and try to start the Sportster, but it won't turn over – out of gas. I put the top up and wait for Haint. When he comes down from the beach, I make him go walk for the gas. Leonora and China Lee head up to the house to freshen up and make some daiquiris. I start on the Suburban's two tires. I cut my hand on the first tire when the jack slips in the sand and spend a good ten minutes looking for a rag and cursing the whole goddamn event. Haint comes back about forty-five minutes later, riding shotgun in a little yellow dune buggy.

A red faced girl in a blue bikini hops out of the car. She is a tall girl, taller than Haint or me, and muscular. She pulls a tank off the back of the buggy. She looks like she knows what she is doing, so I don't offer to help and she manages just fine, lifting the thirty-pound can and pouring the whole load straight into the Mercedes without any funnel. "That's a little over six gallons," she says. Her name is Joleen and her hair

Doug Frelke

keeps blowing against her sunburned cheeks and bleached eyebrows while she talks, in real cute way I think, with little wisps of reddish blond hair shagging around her face. She talks about how the waves are really much better in the winter, flat on top, easy to ride. She asks me if I ever tried surfing before.

"No," I say. "But it sounds like fun." And I shock myself when I hear my own voice say it might be a good thing to try.

Haint works off the second tire and every now and then says something to either Joleen or me. When she walks the empty tank back to her car, Haint says, "I found her up on the beach."

I don't say anything; my damn hand hurts too much. But I can't help but think that Haint makes this look easy too, barely breaking a sweat on the tires.

Haint rolls the two flats over to the dune buggy. Joleen says she'll ride him up to get them patched and filled. "We'll bring back some dinner. Joleen knows a good place to get steaks."

"I'm going to go," I say.

Haint laughs. He thinks I am just trying to push him. And I realize he is right – standing there next to Joleen, with the wind and the sand cutting into my face and the pain in my hand, I am ready to fight him.

Haint looks up to the house. "Good idea, Graham. I'll start the grill. Be back by the time the coals get hot."

"I'll get some beer, too," I say, trying to retreat a little. But I feel huge, climbing in beside Joleen. She sees it too, takes my hand and holds it to the gear shift while we drive. "Feel that, Graham, this little car can move." And she pops the clutch, sending more sand into the air while the tires fin for a moment, before they finally bite and spin true. I see Haint waving in the side view mirror. Then he turns and climbs the pressure-treated stairs.

At the station, Joleen chews gum waiting for tires. I fetch her a Mountain Dew from an old style, dented aluminum ice box in the mechanic's lounge. She has pulled a short salmon sundress over her, and it breaks high on her thighs, shifting in the rising wind. The sun is still warm, but with the wind and the cold drinks, my hands are cold. I put them on the hood of the buggy to warm them.

Joleen crosses over to me. "What are you doing?" She is curious and holds her hair back from her eyes, exposing her high freckled forehead.

I put my warm hand against her forehead. "Warming my hands."

"Let's slide up here." I sit on the peak of the buggy's hood, resting my back against the windshield. Joleen rolls up beside me. "Nice. But it would be better if you put your arm around me, Graham."

And so I do. I hold her close, smelling sweet coconut oil on her neck. The wind pushes her hair across my face and into my open mouth and I taste it – salt and soap. "How are you feeling today, Joleen?" I say.

At the bottom of the stairs, I pause to rub my sore hand – I look out and see the tide beginning to come in. Joleen has run inside with the steaks and beer and has left me time to limp up the stairs by myself. The old sea foam is gone now, either washed back out with the tide or blown further down the beach. Leonora is sitting at the top of the deck, wearing a light green sundress that comes down just above her bare knees. She hands me a daiquiri.

"I know you don't like these sugary drinks, but I thought you might like something cool."

"No. That's fine." I take the drink and sip it – strawberry Kool-Aid and Bacardi. Leonora has her hair down; it's wet and heavy after its combing and sets firmly about her face.

"Where's Haint?," I say.

"He went for a swim and now he's taking a hot shower."

"He's crazy swimming this late in the year. The

45

water will freeze his bones."

Leonora brings her fist to her face, knuckles under her nose. "We're all crazy, Graham. At least about something."

"Yeah." But Leonora knows, better than anyone, I don't believe in that.

She frowns at my hand. "Oh, Graham. You've hurt yourself."

I unwind the rag to show her and she makes a fuss and yells to China Lee to bring out the peroxide and some antiseptic cream. And she cleans it and it stings like hell, but it feels good to have a woman's attention, especially Leonora's. She is tender and asks if it stings and I say no, not really, and she dries my hand very carefully afterwards and applies the cream. "Good as new," she says.

China Lee comes out in her famous halter outfit with the little mini that had been banned from the sales office. But at the beach house it doesn't look so outlandish. Haint wanders out to the deck, with his hair still dripping wet. China Lee chases him with a towel. "You have to dry it Haint or you'll catch pneumonia." I laugh and so does Leonora, while Haint bends down and lets China Lee rub his head with the towel.

"Oww. Leave the ears," Haint says. She rubs once more, then stops. Haint gives China Lee a quick kiss on the cheek. "Thanks."

China Lee puts her arms around his neck. "More," she says, and Haint kisses her again, this time deep and full. Haint sees me and salutes. I salute back.

"How's Joleen?"

"Good."

Leonora gets up and smooths her skirt. "I'm going into the kitchen to help the girls. Call if you need us."

Haint checks the coals. "They look pretty good."

"I'll get the steaks."

"Okay." Haint closes the grill. "Bring some beers, too, will you? This sweet stuff bugs me." He points at his daiquiri glass and makes a sour face.

Push

"Yeah. Ugh." I leave Haint for the steaks, crossing through the slider into the kitchen. China Lee is still in the bathroom and I can hear her talking to herself saying something sweet and quiet, but I can't make it out and decide that I don't really want to. I rift through the cabinets until I find a tray for the steaks and a big steel fork.

Then I sneak back outside.

"Joleen seems to be sold on you," he says.

"So far." I look over my shoulder. The women are in the kitchen microwaving baked potatoes and putting together a salad. They all seem to be talking back and forth about something, and China Lee is laughing at Joleen. I sip my beer. "I keep thinking I'm too old for this stuff, Haint."

Haint sits down in Leonora's deck chair. "Don't think, Graham. Don't think, and you'll be fine."

"You say that like it's an easy thing."

"Easy enough." Haint leans back in the chair. He raises his fist to his lips. "You still mad at me?"

"No. I'm fine." I turn over the steaks; they are going to be well done. "Haint, you know I used to be close with Leonora? We dated before she married E.J."

"Yeah, I know. She told me." He gets up from his chair, stretches. "I think she still likes you, Graham."

"Like and love are different."

"Sure." Haint turns to the glass door. "She's still a fine looking woman though. Prettier than China Lee will ever be."

Haint has named one of my own private thoughts — I have always thought that myself, every time I see them side by side.

"Well, China Lee is still young, you know. Who knows what she'll turn out to be." I turn to see his face, then, to see if he believes me, but he is gone, back inside already.

In the kitchen, the food is crammed end to end along Leonora's makeshift table — a plastic deck table and an old folding card table are pushed together,

47

Doug Frelke

ignoring the inch difference in height. Most of the pots and plates are mismatch, and the five steaks overflow the old tray I pirated, dripping meat juice onto the checked plastic tablecloth. A dozen ears of fresh corn sit in the still warm boiling pot, drained of water. The salad has been mixed up in an old crab pot and sits over beside the stove, two metal serving spoons hanging out of the top. There are no shakers, so China Lee has put the cylinder of Morton's salt right in the middle of the table, along with a measuring cup of melted butter and a pint of sour cream. Everything seems Jack-And-the-Beanstalk sized; my face feels red, flushed.

    Haint and I take our steaks and split a third; Joleen has a smaller one with two potatoes, and even Leonora and China Lee split the last one, though they don't like to eat meat. China Lee fetches the salad and doles it out right on top of the steaks – lettuce and scallions, sliced mushrooms and fresh tomatoes, cucumbers and little bits of ham. Leonora passes around salad dressing, Ranch and Italian. Joleen divvies up the potatoes, and I get two. I split both in half and cover them with sour cream and salt. Haint opens a bottle of Chianti from the kitchen, and we all have a glass of that, with our beer and the girls' daiquiris.

    I watch Joleen cut her steak; she stabs dainty pieces moving them around her plate like a sponge, soaking up the extra meat juice and salad dressing from the corners of her plate. China Lee offers to make more daiquiris, and Haint goes out to finish up the extra steaks. He and I stuff them down, too, even though they are pretty rare. Still, when Joleen brings out a lemon meringue pie, we all have to eat a fair sized slice. We wander out to the couches in the den, and collapse into long lazy folds with our feet stuck out onto the glass coffee table, pushing the seashell ashtrays and old magazines to the floor.

    I stick my head deep into one of the pillows, smelling mildew and sand and salt. Joleen comes over from the table and lays beside me, puts her head in my lap. I

Push

rub her ear, gently running the thumb of my good hand along its curves, brushing her hair to the side.

    Leonora brings me over another beer, then sits down next to Haint. China Lee sits on Haint's lap, holding his hand and tracing his fingers in quiet lines with her nails. We stay like that for about an hour, full and resting. Then China Lee has to get up to make coffee – all three of the women worry about us driving home. When China Lee gets up, Leonora slides right over to Haint's lap, straightening her green dress around her knees. Then she takes up his hand and locks it between the two of her own.

    After the coffee, I hate like hell to go and try to stretch back out on the couch, but Haint gets up for the door, giving me a final call. He kisses China Lee, a long kiss, and then one for Leonora, too. I don't watch that one, instead I am kissing Joleen and she is kissing me back and when I let her go she grabs my neck and kisses me again. "I like you, Graham," she says and I say I like you too Joleen, I really do.

    We leave the three of them standing out near Joleen's dune buggy; they wave and blow kisses, as Haint makes elaborate circles in the sandy road. Then we shoot off, streaming past the unlit rows of empty beach houses.

    We drive a good way into the night and the wind dies down and we decide to lower the top at the first gas station. Haint goes in and brings out two cokes for the road, both still dripping water from the ice bucket where he plucked them, and I hold mine in my bad hand feeling the kind coolness of it. The moon is out and full, slung low. The moon sits so low, it seems as if we could drive to it and then pass on by, like any other well lit sign along the road.

    We drive. I ask Haint if he wants me to take a turn but he says no he is fine and everything is fine. Then I ask him how long he has been sleeping with Leonora.

    "About two months, Graham."

    "And China Lee?"

Doug Frelke

"Roughly the same." Haint's eyes remain on the road, tracing the yellow dashes of the divider. He doesn't look over to me, though I wait to see if he might, before I speak.

"Why the hell would you do a thing like that, Haint?"

"To be fair."

"Ha. Well, I think it's a damn shame."

Haint nods. "What if I was to say Leonora asked me to, Graham?" He reaches down to open his coke. "What would you think then?"

"I wouldn't think a damn thing about that. I wouldn't believe you."

"No. I didn't think you would. People believe what they want to, Graham. You should know that."

"The truth doesn't make any difference?"

"I don't know, Graham. I don't think about the truth." Haint raises the coke to his lips, drinks. "What the fuck is the truth anyway?"

Haint reaches over to the middle section of the car, flips open the armrest. "Look," he says. Haint holds up a lipstick. He takes the cap off, throws it over his shoulder. He rolls out a quarter inch of the red wax. He pokes it at me, slow like he is trying to mark me. I move away, shooing his hand.

"Watch." The road has divided now and there are a few arc lights shining down on the beginnings of a new road – concrete barriers divide off the construction with orange blinkers every hundred yards. Haint passes one of the blinkers and slows the car; he down shifts and swings the car to the left, a quick swerve – two feet from the concrete rail. He shoves his left hand out; the lipstick touches the concrete as he drives, rolling out a long red vibrant smear under the arc lights. The next blinker closes in, a water barrier in front. Haint's red line skips, retreats, as the tube runs out; then, sparks, as the concrete reaches the metal of the tube. Haint holds the tube for a second longer like a kid with a sparkler then he pulls hard to the right, and the back left tire

Push

thumps over the scored concrete lead.

Haint drops the marred tube to the road. "Ouch," he says. "The damn thing gets hot." And then we are through the construction and the arc lights and the blinkers, and the road is just an old country road again, moonlight hitting the concrete and shining like water.

"That's your problem, Graham. You aren't willing to live close in. That's what life is – burns and stains and hurt, mixed in with all the glory."

Haint nods his head, like he is talking to himself. "Graham, you are forty-seven years old. You have about ten years before you're on the real downward slope, maybe fifteen, but probably not, based on your diet and everything. So we're back to ten goddamn years. When are you going to live, Graham?"

"You don't do things, Haint, just because you can."

"Sure you do, Graham. Look at E.J. Look at Leonora and China Lee, for God's sake. Everything is there to be done – to be taken, eaten used. Me, you, them, the money, the job, Joleen – everything."

I don't say anything for a while. I raise my fist to hit him, right across the mouth as he looks dead at the road. I could have hit him then, and maybe I would have killed him, maybe I would have killed myself, too, if he would have let go of the wheel and lost control of the car. But I didn't hit him then.

"This life of ours is a peach, Graham. Joleen – that was something right, that kiss? You do what you want, but I'm going to eat the whole fucking peach, Graham. The whole goddamn thing. And when I die, it'll be from choking on the pit."

Haint screws the top back on his coke, shoves it under his seat. "Truth? That old woman I sold the Cadillac to – she's my mother's aunt. I've known her since I was a baby. A set up, Graham. Truth."

I hit him then, my left fist hard to his jaw. The car swerves and Haint winces, looking over. But Haint knew it was coming, he expected it by then. No loss of control, no real damage done.

51

Doug Frelke

"Yeah." I say. I feel sick, taste kool-aid and rum under my tongue. I am cold; I huddle down in the seat to be near the heater. We drive the last twenty miles back to Jefferson motors. I get in my car then and go home. I leave Haint to raise the top of the sportster.

It's a funny thing about being right. It never makes you feel that damn good really. The best you feel is relief at not being wrong.

In early February, we came in and Haint was gone. He took the petty cash, about three grand, but even E.J. couldn't begrudge him that – we already owed him that much in commission. Because Haint never slowed down on the selling end; until the day he left, he was closing deals and we were all closing deals and making the same sick money we were beginning to expect with him around.

Florida was gone too, with her little red Pacer, and the word was that Haint had gone with her out West. But there were lots of side theories – E.J. and Reed were pretty determined that Haint had headed South all on his own, to start up his own place.

I had given up thinking by that time, so I didn't say a damn thing.

In March, Leonora asked E.J. for a divorce. She and China Lee had decided to move North, so China Lee could finish out her senior year and get into a decent college.

The shocker was that Leonora was pregnant. When E.J. found that out, he came after me with a tire iron and such wild fury that I thought he would surely kill me. But even he could see I was as knocked by the news as he was, and in the end, that kept him from killing me. Instead, he beat a two-foot hole in the side of his office and threw his chair through the glass wall. I watched as it rolled out into Dickinson avenue, streaming crystals of safety glass.

After that, E.J. would sit at China Lee's desk inside the office. Reed went to work for another lot down the

Push

street, and he did pretty well selling Hyundais and Nissans. He had watched Haint, close, learning. Reed was smarter than either me or E.J. ever gave him credit.

I'm still at the lot. I sell a car or two and sometimes when I really have it working I feel like I'm living. But, I have adapted to being small again. There are still times when I feel huge and brimming, like at the end of a good sale. I am thankful that it doesn't linger; just small risings on a downward slope.

And I'm glad I'm no longer a thinking man, because if I was, it would kill me thinking about Haint all the time.

Still, thinking is a hard habit to break.

Sometimes I catch myself, while watching the cars move back and forth on Dickinson Avenue. What Haint said – ten years, tick-tock. And the big surf. A blue bikini and a hard french kiss and everything as big as the moon. Eat the peach.

Living With the Magician

When she sees her father like this, with his straight blond hair swinging wild and his hands raised high, she imagines him as a Baptist preacher. He sounds religious, though his voice is inconsistent; a long shout and then soft to mumbles, but she listens. "We walk in heavy shoes. Our shoes are too heavy," he says.

He wears light tan corduroys, a white shirt, the kind of clothes he always wears, whites and khakis and greys, that allow him to fade away in front of you; and though he is six foot two, he is almost invisible, as if you could lose him in the sun if you turned away. That is more of the magic in him, that invisibility.

"Fish. Fishes. We are God's own flesh, his fish. His own fleshy fish." But he is a salesman by trade; that has always perplexed her. Here he speaks, and his nonsense words still echo like a salesman – convincing, tempting. Once he had been elected president of his senior class. She can see that in him, too, at times like these.

Jackson Teal's voice keeps getting louder, carrying across the linoleum floor in echoes and ricochets, crawling into the ears of the twenty patients, the one nurse, the

Living With the Magician

two nurse assistants. The Burlington Dialysis Center has a temporary feel to it, like it could be packed up and moved off tomorrow; IVs hang from every extra hook, and dozens of small metal tables have been pushed here and there on broken wheels and crammed with medication and kool-aid packs, medical tape, gauze, old *People* magazines. Dust covered fluorescents send out worn light in well beaten tracks; black streaks crisscross the old white floor, showing the passage of the thick wheels of the dialysis machines. There are blue curtains closing off each machine – they provide some privacy to the patients, who are splayed out in a semicircle of second hand easy chairs. The patients sit close to the machines because they are physically attached to them – by shunts and needles and tubes – but also as if they were sitting near a fire for warmth. The machines are the miracle; eight-foot banks of turning centifuges that pop off a tight dialogue of bips and whirs as they work their own magic of new clean blood.

"There will be no more pain. There will be no more suffering. I will cure you." My father makes a wide gesture with his hands, as if he is trying to grasp them all in his arms; the tubes from his machine jangle and twist, like so much jewelry. He wobbles, speaks some more, sinks down into whispers. His shoes scuff back and forth trying to find a hold on the waxed floor.

Some of the patients smile at my father, a few look down at their feet or off down the hall, embarrassed. No one listens to him for real.

"You go, Mr. Jack. You do your thing." Julio, the male nurse assistant, comes to my father's side. "It's just the sugar. We will get you straight." But Julio is more of a mop pusher than a nurse; he doesn't know anything but what he's heard from the other nurses. He picks up a cheap butter cookie, a hundred in a cardboard box. My father slaps his hand away.

"I am straight. I am an arrow to heaven." He grasps Julio's arm with a shaky, rapid fire hand. "Straight!"

But my father's eyes give him away. He cannot focus

Doug Frelke

when he is high – you are too bright, he has said to me in the past – he must always cut his gaze away from you. No one else can get as high as my father can; it is the one thing that he can still do better than anyone. He's diabetic, and if the dialysis machine pulls him too hard, his blood sugar crashes. As it goes lower he goes higher, just like that. Only if it stays low, he could go into shock, which he has done before. Or he could fall into a coma, and die.

"Here. I'll do it." I take two cookies, dip them in the weak red kool-aid beside him. "Here. This is God food. Eat it."

He smiles. Opens his mouth wide, chews. "Good," he says. "I'm God. So is he." My father points to Julio.

"Thanks, Mr. Jack. But they don't pay me enough to be a God around here." Julio winks at the other patients.

Mrs. Mallory is sixty, blind and fat – she squeezes her blind eyes shut as she laughs. "You are so funny, Julio. But he can't help it. Least he isn't calling us names." She talks coy with Julio; her blind old eyes still see herself as she was thirty years ago – when she had bobbed black hair and wore silk and lace and men would pay good money to be with her. Mrs. Mallory was never a whore – I've heard Doctor Pope say that to the men, Julio, Leroy, my father. But she had friends. Enough so she can still afford to have a taxi pick her up and take her home from her dialysis three days a week.

Doctor Pope shakes his head. "You people do not understand the nature of illness. He does what he is forced to do." Even at eighty-five, Doctor Pope still holds himself tightly, with a hard old southern whiteness that is in his hair oil and his long fingers with their ever-clean nails. He looks ready for his next surgery, though he has not practiced medicine in almost fifteen years.

But he is right about my father. My father is forced to do almost everything by his illness – when he gets high he curses them, has even taken swings at Julio. Julio has not forgotten. My father called him a "little faggot," though he is close to three hundred pounds and makes

Living With the Magician

eyes at all the women, even me. He called Mrs. Mallory a "blue whore," so she does not like my father now. "Why blue?" She had asked Doctor Pope.

Doctor Pope has tolerance for my father because he is also a diabetic, though he is quick to point out they have different strains and his is better, less severe. He has even invited my father to his house. My father went out there to sell him a white Pontiac, and they sat on his porch in pine rockers and drank Mint Juleps brought to them by the old black man Doctor Pope keeps as his butler. The whole afternoon was old timey Southern, my father said. Not in a bad way, but more like everyone was play acting – my father, Dr. Pope, even the black butler with his "Yes, suhs," and "No, suhs."

Julio says Doctor Pope was a leader of the Ku Klux Klan back in the sixties; but my father says he never heard that. And Doctor Pope frequently points out Julio's mistakes, like when he put the wrong IV in Leroy's arm and had to pull it out and try to find the vein all over again.

Leroy watches my father closely. He does not know whether he should try to help or brace himself for protection. He is black, in his thirties. Leroy is very quiet with his sickness, but I do not know if that is his nature or if it's because he is the only black in a room full of whites. Even Julio, who is Mexican, isn't black. In my part of North Carolina, there's black and white. Everything else – Mexican, Indian, Chinese – is too foreign to count.

The nurse, Peggy, arrives from the other side of the clinic. She pulls the curtain aside, sticks her head in the room. Her blond hair hangs loose and her mascara has begun to run. She does not enter. "You're doing fine, Melanie. Keep him eating. He'll be fine." I wave her off; I know what to do. She can go help someone else.

Peggy lets the curtain close. "If you need any help, I'll come back."

My father will not remember any of this. He is two people now – the one I take home, barely able to move, and this wild momentary force. He nods when I tell him,

Doug Frelke

and sometimes he winces, like with Julio being a faggot. He does not ask questions – he does not want to know anything about the man that says all those things. "The Magician," my father calls him. Because we do not know when he will appear or what he will do when he does.

Once he comes down, he is just my father again. A young old man with his bad kidneys and his diabetes, selling cars to his ex-high school crowd and their growing families. He is thirty-seven years old and he sleeps fifteen hours a day.

"She is so good with him," I hear Mrs. Mallory's voice. "It must be very hard for her." Blind people have a perfect volume; they know exactly what is heard. "What does she look like?" she says.

Julio answers. "Melanie? Like an hijo; short hair – colored purple. She has a ring in her nose, holes in her ears."

"She does not have purple hair, Julio. It must be red."

"It's purple. Short like a boy, but with all those earrings."

"You're so funny, Julio. I'm sure she is the prettiest little thing."

I am fourteen, almost fifteen. To hell with them. To hell with Julio, three hundred pounds, and the old blue whore. I do what I want.

Julio's son is named Diego. He's sixteen. He waits for me outside, offers me a cigarette, lights it when I accept. He likes me, wants me to go for a ride with him in his old spick Firebird. He's just had it painted, he tells me, and had a new stereo put in. Before the paint job, the car used to be a farty old brown with a jacked up back end and huge tires. My father had sold him the car.

"What color?"

"Orange. Like fire."

"Orange. Like an piece of fruit," I say. "Why'd you get orange?"

Diego shrugs. "It was closeout. I had my cousin paint it." I figure he bought the stereo from his cousin, too. It

Living With the Magician

probably was stolen in a yank job, so it doesn't have any knobs left and he will have to tune in the stations with a screwdriver.

Diego is big like his father, chunky and heavy armed, but not quite fat; he has a wide flat face with acne in stripes under his eyes and across his forehead. He wants to get an earring and asks me if it hurts much.

"It's easy." I say. "The skin is dead. You probably won't even bleed."

He nods. "A diamond," he says, pinches his ear. "That is what I will get."

"Yeah, that would look tough." But tough boys don't ask if it will hurt. And Julio would kill him. Which is why I like to encourage Diego about the earring.

"You want to go for a drive?"

"Maybe next time. My dad had a bad day. I need to see him home."

Diego nods. "Your dad is tough. Julio says he's the toughest one he's ever seen." Diego shakes out a cigarette. "Here, take one for later."

And I feel bad then, but I take it; I make a note to take a ride with him in his old orange crap car once. We can take the back roads where no one will see me.

My father gets to our Duster with Julio's help. He lies down in the back. I get out my phone book for the seat, tilt in the steering wheel, slide up as close as I can to the pedals.

"You drive this thing all right? I could get Diego to drive him home." Julio grins. He says that every week.

"No, I'm fine. It's just five miles."

"Okay, girl. See you Wednesday." He waves. I kick at the clutch and shift on the column, first to second, again for second to third. We are moving. My father snores softly from the rear seat. We will be back on Wednesday – then Friday, then Sunday, then Tuesday, then Thursday. For as long as my father can stand it.

When I get home, I roll about halfway up the drive way and cut left through the high grass of the front yard.

59

Doug Frelke

Our neighbors watch from their windows. The car leaves thick brown streaks in the grass – a big car like that on the soft grass – but what can you do? I get as close as I can to the front step. We have a walker, and if he'd use it I wouldn't have to park so close. But he fell one time, and refuses to touch it again. My father is used to falling in public places. He is used to people watching him while pretending to be looking in store windows or scolding their children. But with the walker, it was just too pitiful.

He's half asleep and six pounds lighter with the water weight sucked out of him; I can manage him myself. One hand around my neck, the other grasping the rail, the edge of the door, the inside stairs. He feels his way across our ripped green rug. Once we get inside he will crawl if he has to, to get to his bed. His bedroom is on the first floor, about twenty feet from the car door.

I take off his shoes, unbuckle his pants and put them on a hanger. He is already asleep. I like to see him this way – peaceful, stretched long across the bed, so you can see his tallness and the good muscles he still has in his arms and chest. He is handsome even; in the dark he could be eighteen, and he sleeps with his hands folded under his chest like he is holding something close to his heart as he dreams.

My father once said we are treating ourselves now, said it when he was straight and sick, trying to eat his spaghetti dinner at our kitchen table without throwing up too much. I liked that, we are treating ourselves. I think it is true, with him and me. I unzip my boots, kick them into the corner of the room. I finger out each earring, placing them in a little cup on the bedside table. I slip out of my jeans and bra, drop my underwear and T-shirt in a ball. I walk into the bathroom and look at myself in the mirror, naked. I scrub my teeth and brush my hair. I should let it grow out, and maybe dye it blond, like mother's. When I am done, I go back into the bedroom and climb in next to him.

My father never picked his women very well – they

Living With the Magician

are too much like his cars, fast and shiny, expensive. I love my mother, but I could see what was going to happen. She lives out on the beach now, and she calls on Sunday mornings. Sometimes she speaks to him, and I used to hear him say he loved her, missed her. He does not say that to her now; he says hardly anything at all and makes excuses to keep her from visiting.

Around ten PM, I get up to make us something to eat. He has to get up and eat, though he normally doesn't want to, still sick from the dialysis. So I make something easy, hotdogs with macaroni and cheese. Walking around the kitchen naked, I feel the heat of the day breaking, the sun finally giving itself up. I open the window, waiting for the microwave to finish. I bring his bowl to the bed, sit down beside him.

"Melanie. You should put on some clothes," he says. There is a long shelf over his bed for anything he might need – Tums, insulin, a plastic carafe for his urine test. He takes a white tee-shirt from the shelf, pulls it over the goose bumps along his arms.

"Maybe I like being naked."

"I know you like being naked." He tries to lean forward some, so he can eat.

"Can you eat this? I could make you something else."

"Yeah, it's fine. I'm fine. Why don't you put some clothes on? It's cold."

"It's eighty degrees."

"Oh." He is surprised by that – that he is so cold and it is eighty degrees. I get up, slide on my jeans without any underwear, put on my tee-shirt. "There is a bit of a breeze. I'll close the window."

"Thanks. Sorry."

"You should have seen yourself today. You were something. You thought you were God. You said Julio was too."

"Well, he had to like that I guess."

"Yeah, you weren't too bad today. Just funny. You kept talking about fishes and shoes. Why do you think you said that stuff?"

Doug Frelke

"I don't know, Hon. I don't know what the magician does. I don't feel like a god. The way I feel today, I could be dead by the end of the week."

"Don't say that."

"I don't mean it. I just feel like hell."

"Sure. Eat and then sleep. I'll be here if you need anything."

"I need to go into the bathroom."

"I'll help you."

"All right, but I think I can make it mostly."

I follow behind him, making sure he doesn't trip. He gets in, calls for me to help him up when he is done. I get him back to the bed, tuck him in. I am not ready to sleep. I go out to do the dishes, watch some TV. I think about him; I always come back to thinking about him. When it first happened between us, he had that look like after the magician; he thought it was terrible. But me, I felt like everything was working out right for once. It makes me laugh when I think about it – what this whole world puts you through and then it tries to tell you there are rules. I think about what Dr. Pope and Mrs. Mallory and Julio would say if they knew. What Leroy or Diego would say. But it doesn't touch me. I do what I want.

I try to be realistic, though, think how long he will live – two years, at most five. So I will be sixteen to nineteen when he dies. I need to give him something more. Tomorrow, I will start to grow my hair out, and when it gets long and full, I'll dye it blond. That will be something for him; he has always liked blondes. These are the things I can still do for him. I feed him. I touch him. I love him. I do what I want.

Smoke

Joe rubs his face, turning the ash coating on his cheeks from grey to black. The ash is everywhere, on everything. Out here, they eat their food quickly, so they do not swallow too much of it, and they drink their water from canteens. Still the food and water have a burnt taste that stays on their tongues.

Joe sits on the minesweeper's fantail. His ship is clearing passage on a five mile route off the coast of Kuwait City. At night when the ship is at the start of the route, you can see the outline of the port – navigation lights and airport signals rich, clear lights. Even the twin spire landmark of the city, still standing, is lined with bright yellow bulbs. But by the five mile point on the track, the smoke has become so thick it is it's own presence, and you must use the charts to make your turn, even in the daylight hours. The smoke is like a cloud of moon dust or prehistoric gas. It provides a kind of timelessness, a lack of any real location. Here everything changes in relation to the smoke.

Joe thinks of home – he is afraid of going home, so the time remaining on the ship has become precious to him; he counts the days and hours with a kind of

Doug Frelke

mourning. His wife, Sheryl, left him right before he came to the Gulf; Joe does not know how he will stand it, being alone in their old house with closets and drawers full of her things. He hopes that she has come back and taken every stick of furniture – the pictures on the walls, even his things – his best hope is that the house will be empty, so nothing will remain to remind him.

His two companions wander over to join him, going through their standard motions before they will sit, like a pair of old dogs lying down. Hubbard leans over the side and spits into the ship's wake; Johnson pats his chest for his lighter and fingers a fresh pack of Marlboros.

"Three more weeks," Johnson says. He is young and scared and his words sparkle with trust and hope, sticking in his throat as he speaks.

"Three damn weeks," Hubbard says. His full name is Baxter Hubbard and he is older, bald, affecting a tired air. And yet the crew calls him Mother and means it and he gives them a shove or a push when they say it but he loves it all the same. And Baxter Hubbard will miss the cruise when it is over, more than any of them.

"Then home," Joe says, finishing the thought for them.

They turn to Joe. No one else is on the fantail to listen – the rest of the crew gives the three of them, the Mine Detail, a natural distance. The other men fear the smoke, the mines in the water, the threat of dying out here. So they avoid the reminder, the Mine Detail. But when the Sonar Technicians find a mine, all the others sweep up onto the decks and line the rail as the Mine Detail climbs down into the ship's small boat to mark the mine for the divers. They are ready to do their job then – Mother flashing the finger to the deck hands, Johnson testing the knots on the anchor line, Joe concentrating on the engine. The officers stand on the main deck and wave colored flashlights, directing them north, south, port, starboard. All three are volunteers.

Smoke

Joe smiles. "There's this guy. He's a lion tamer."

"Ha!" Johnson, sits above the other two, perched on the rail. He brushes a cowlick of blond hair out of his eyes. "Just got a care package from my wife. Fresh American Marlboros." Johnson lights one, blows out his match. He lays his cigarette on the edge of the rail, strikes another match and lights theirs, one, two, both dangling from his mouth. He puffs once to make sure they are lit before he passes them over to Baxter, then to Joe.

Johnson volunteered for the Mine Detail for the extra pay; he wants to build his wife a house when he gets back home to Mount Pleasant, South Carolina. He talks about the house all the time – it will be made of red brick with a wraparound white porch. Mount Pleasant is in hurricane country, and Johnson wants to make sure he builds something that will hold the ground.

Joe holds the cigarette to his nose, breathing in the full scent of the tobacco, molasses, and clean paper. "Thanks," he says. "So this lion tamer's afraid to go to sleep."

Hubbard blows out misshapen smoke rings. "You forget about American cigarettes. You get used to always smoking stale stuff or foreign shit that tastes like erasers." Hubbard looks at Johnson, but his eyes are on Joe. They both are attentive now, Joe's voice beginning to register. He is telling them something, a story.

"For the last month, every time he's tried to sleep he's had the same awful nightmare. And it scares him so bad he can't even think about going back to sleep."

Joe smokes his cigarette, slowly, trying to get the taste; but his mouth is so burnt from the smoke that he can't be sure if he is tasting anything real or just remembering how a fresh cigarette should taste. "In the nightmare, the lion tamer is in the big top doing his act, wearing his gold costume and flicking his rawhide whip at the lions – just like a regular night. He begins the

Doug Frelke

finale of his act, where he dances a waltz with his favorite lioness, Sheba, while the other lions sit on their haunches and watch. In the dream, though, Sheba attacks him."

Hubbard laughs. "That's what you get for fucking with lions." Baxter Hubbard had volunteered for the Mine Detail to get his First Class stripe back – he had been busted to Second for breaking a Marine's jaw in Abu-Dhabi. And Joe can see that in him, how his life is simple – just action and reaction. And Joe is jealous in a way.

Johnson clicks the toe of his work boot against the side of Hubbard's head, just above his ear. "Shut the hell up, Hubbard. I'm listening to Joe's story."

Hubbard smacks the boot with his fist. "To hell with you, Johnson. I can say what I want." He flicks his finished cigarette over his shoulder, towards Johnson. "And if you don't like it, I'll kick your ass."

Johnson looks to Joe. "I want to hear the story."

Joe nods. "Sheba attacks the lion tamer. And the lion tamer is forced to fight back, breaking his whip against the side of her jaw. And that buys him enough time to limp across the cage to the door."

The smoke has faded with the day. Out behind Johnson's head it is all darkness now with the sunset, and though Johnson and Hubbard are only five feet from him, Joe can only see them by their rough black shapes and the ember of their cigarettes. "Every night the dream ends the same for the lion tamer. As soon as he puts his hand on the latch, as soon as he can feel that iron bar in his hand, the whole pride is on him. And they sink their teeth into him."

Johnson says, "I hate this place."

Mother lights another cigarette and the momentary flash emphasizes the shadows on his face, like a jack-o'-lantern. "Yeah, this is like being nowhere. Six months and not one day that's clear enough to see the horizon."

Joe nods. Before Johnson and Hubbard joined him

Smoke

on the fantail, he had been reading a letter. It was an old letter, one Sheryl wrote to him almost five years ago – just a list of work projects she wanted him to do over the summer. An herb garden. Clearing a long stretch along the back for sunflower plants. Pouring a concrete path from the porch to the street. He brought the letter with him because it summons her to him in her choice of phrases, like "hoe the weeds," and "turn the soil," – a farmer's daughter in a farmer's town, betraying her own understanding and his need to be instructed.

"Doesn't matter," Joe says. "Can't see the mines anyhow." Hubbard and Johnson are silent; they know that Joe has been in the Persian Gulf before – as part of Operation Safe Pass in 1992. Joe got out of the Navy after that. But with the war, he volunteered for a six month tour. He is from Persimmon Gap, West Texas. He is a good sailor, and they trust him, even like him most of the time. But they both wonder why Joe is here. Why would a man come back to this place if he knew it?

They sit in the dark, silent, smoking their cigarettes. Finally, Baxter Hubbard speaks, "The lion tamer, Joe."

Joe looks out towards the voice. "Yeah. Sure. So the lion tamer can't sleep because of the nightmare. He knows he can't remain awake by himself, so he invents a game to help him. On the first night, he finds a seat in a bar and every time someone comes in, the lion tamer swaggers up to the new guy, and he says, 'I'll bet you ten to one I can drink you under the table.' So these guys play the game with the lion tamer. By the end of the first night, the lion tamer has beaten everyone he can find, and he's got a thick stack of ones sitting next to him.

"The lion tamer comes back the next night, only no one will play him. By then, everyone realizes it is a sucker's bet, even at ten to one. So the lion tamer raises the odds to one hundred to one.

"At those odds, a few more players come forward. By the end of the second night, the lion tamer has

67

Doug Frelke

beaten everyone again, but his stack of ones has barely grown at all.

"On the third night, the lion tamer can't find any takers for his bet, and he begins to get nervous that he will fall asleep. So he raises the odds to a thousand to one.

"A rich banker comes up to the lion tamer. The banker says, 'Son, I've made my living biding my time until the odds are in my favor. I'll play you.'

"The banker starts off fast, getting a one shot lead on the lion tamer. But the lion tamer is steady and catches up. By three AM, the banker is behind and knows he's beat.

"The banker lays his dollar on the table. He says, 'You know, that's some feat of drinking, boy. But I'm a successful businessman, and I'm telling you there's no hope for you getting rich this way. Even if you beat a hundred men, the one hundred and first will get you.'

"The lion tamer just takes the banker's dollar and smiles. He says, 'I don't think about the money; I never ask the ringmaster how much I'll make before a show. If I thought about money when I was in the ring, I might forget to remember that lions have sharp claws. And then those claws would slice right through me.'"

Hubbard says, "Ha. I like that story, Joe. I hate bankers."

Joe turns towards Hubbard's voice. He sees Johnson, who has bent down until his head is framed just slightly above Hubbard's. Joe watches as Johnson touches the edge of his cigarette to Hubbard's ear.

"Goddamn!" Hubbard jumps up, his hand shooting to his ear.

Johnson giggles, his voice rising in pitch. "I got you, Mother. I fucking got you." He kicks his boot at Hubbard.

Hubbard catches his boot and shoves Johnson over the rail. His arms lock around Johnson's calf, holding him. "How do you like that, you dumb son of a bitch!"

Johnson kicks his free foot at Baxter Hubbard's

Smoke

face; his boot connects, once, twice. "Go ahead and drop me!"

"I should drop you, you little fuck. You almost burned off my damn ear!"

Upside down, Johnson yells, "Do it! Do it, then! Fuck you, Mother! Do it!"

But Mother holds on. Joe gets the kicking foot in his own grasp, and the two of them pin Johnson to the rail. After a minute, Johnson settles.

Joe says, "Okay, Baxter. Let's get him up."

Up close, Joe can see Baxter Hubbard's face – there is a bit of red in the corner of his mouth, and when he talks there is blood on his teeth. "I should have let him drop."

But Baxter Hubbard helps Joe haul Johnson in. And they sit Johnson against the bulkhead, away from the rail.

There are tears in Johnson's eyes, then rolling down his face; when he speaks his voice sounds hollow, recorded. "We're going to die here. Out there in that fog bringing up a mine, or we'll hit one in route. I know it." He sobs, and Joe and Mother look away.

"Why didn't you just do it, Mother?" He runs his hands down his thighs, cleans them on the fabric of his coveralls.

Baxter Hubbard looks at his hands, then at the oil fires lining the horizon. He does not look at Johnson. He says, "You aren't going to die, Johnson. We aren't going to die here. Joe's a ringer – the best coxswain in the whole fucking Navy. Aren't you, Joe?"

Joe sits back down. He smiles. "I am pretty good." Then he leans forward toward Johnson and lowers his voice, as if he is disclosing something secret. "We'll be home in three weeks, Johnson. And then you can build your nice brick house, and your wife can cook us a great big dinner with fried chicken and corn on the cob, and you and Mother and me will all get drunk out on your porch, drinking cold beer and laughing about this place – how easy it was, and how fast the time flew."

Doug Frelke

There's a picture in Johnson's head then – of his house, the red bricks, his wife in a little blue sun dress, sitting on the steps and shucking the corn. "You think?" Johnson says.

"Oh yeah," Joe says.

"Hell, yeah," Baxter Hubbard says. He reaches into his shirt, kisses his crucifix. "Pray to God."

Neither Baxter Hubbard, nor Joe, nor Johnson speak. After a minute, Johnson gets out his Marlboros, fiddles with the matches. He lights another set of three, with two matches as before. Baxter Hubbard passes the first one over to Joe. "Why don't you finish your story, Joe?"

"Yeah," Johnson says, "Finish the story, Joe."

Joe nods, but there is no point in continuing the story. He is still thinking about Johnson's house – the red bricks, Johnson's wife sitting on the porch. The scene is stuck in his head, as if it were real.

"Do you have a light?" The blond woman in the Dallas airport bar sets her margarita down and slides onto the stool beside Joe. Her red miniskirt rides up high on her tanned thighs. She smells of gin and cigarette smoke and her features are all geometry – long nose and jutting cheek bones, a pointed chin. She is like one of those starvation victims, Joe thinks. Her clothes are tight, the red mini and a white tube top, and that too, makes him wonder – that she could find any clothes to fit her thinness so tightly. The only big part of the woman is her mouth – she has an enormous mouth, edged thickly with peach lipstick.

"Thank God you smoke," she says. "Everyone else here has been giving me the evil eye."

There are a dozen people sitting in the bar, coming in to sit or getting up to leave, but none of them seem to be watching Joe or the woman as she sits down. Their eyes are focused on the blue flight monitor in the corner of the bar or the two muted TVs showing basketball and MTV. But Joe knows no one in the bar is watching

Smoke

anything really; they are just waiting for the time to tick by so they can catch their plane and move on, just like he is.

Joe strikes his lighter and the woman leans in close; he sees down into the little scoop of her breasts, sees that they are sunburnt and deep freckled. A topless sun bather, he thinks, catches himself smiling, imagining her so thin and small and flat that he would not even know she was a woman on one of those beaches. He laughs because he has been to one of those beaches, in France, and this is the exact kind of woman he saw sunbathing topless there — flat chested, bony, severe tan. It was a joke to him and the other sailors, then, so different from what they had imagined.

Sheryl had long blond hair, almost white, that she normally wore in a single thick braid. She was wide through the hips, big in the chest, long freckled legs.

"My name is Liz," she says.

"I'm Joe. Pleased to meet you, Liz." He extends his hand. She grasps it with a strong shake and her silver bracelets bang and jangle.

"It's nice to meet you too, Joe." Liz's eyes are black and small — bird's eyes. But they are not mean or hard; they are softer and less sharp than any of her other features. She puffs her cigarette quickly, and Joe knows this is her game — she is not smoking.

"I see you're not married. Or at least not wearing a ring." Joe moves his hand off the bar then, to his lap. Liz laughs, as if she has tricked him into revealing something secret.

"No. I'm still married. We're separated."

"How long?"

"About a year."

"Well that's nice — you being true blue and all." Liz's black eyes move over Joe's face, as though measuring, gauging. "Must be hard, huh?"

"I'd rather not talk about her, really."

"All right." Liz runs her matching peach nails over the back of Joe's hand, up through the hair on his arm.

Doug Frelke

"Want to see my scar?"

Joe smiles. There is something about Liz, not knowing what she will do next, that he likes. She would be doing this with anyone, Joe thinks, and that is comforting, relaxes him.

A clock hangs over the bar, between the two TVs; he sees he has time still, before his flight. "Okay," he says. "Show me your scar."

Liz slides off the stool, stands. She faces away from him. "Okay, watch." Liz turns her head, slashes him a grin over her shoulder. "You'll have to be quick though."

Liz runs her mini skirt zipper up the side of her thigh; she lifts the freed corner with her left hand, while she works the white elastic band of her panties down with her right. And Joe sees. A purple scar high on her left butt cheek, nearly three-inches long. The shape of a shark's tooth.

"I see it," Joe says. Liz re-zips leisurely, smooths the red leather.

"I got bit by a dog when I was a kid." Liz looks at him. "It's a cliché really. Everyone thinks it's funny when I tell them, a dog biting me in the ass and all. But it isn't funny when it's your ass. Is it?"

"No. I don't think so." Joe smashes his cigarette into the ashtray, lights another.

Liz takes the straw from her frozen margarita, licks it with the tip of her tongue. Then she lifts the glass to her mouth and tries to swallow the remaining quarter of her drink. Joe watches her; she tilts her head back, shakes the drink into her open mouth.

"Ohhh!" Liz slams the glass to the bar. She shivers, and her bracelets chime.

The edges of Liz's lips are purple and her nose and cheeks have gone white.

"I don't think I could do that," Joe says.

"I've got a big mouth." Liz flashes her smile. "My dentist says I have thirty-six teeth. That's four more than most people." She takes a napkin, folds it in half,

Smoke

presses it between her lips. "See, Joe." She spreads the napkin on the bar, tracing her finger along the lipstick outline she has created.

"But I'm cold now." She takes his arm and rubs it hard, as if he were the one who had just said he was cold. "Get me something that will warm me, Joe." Liz opens her purse, for her lipstick and a compact.

"Want to hear a story?" Joe says.

"Sure. Anything you want, Joe. But buy me a drink."

"Yeah, all right." Joe motions the bartender, "Two Johnny Walker Reds, please." Liz rotates the stool until she is facing him, attentive.

Joe puts his cigarette in the lip of the ashtray, letting it burn itself down. "There's this lion tamer. He comes to the same bar each night to try to stay awake, because he is afraid to sleep, afraid of his dreams. So he plays a game with the bar's customers, betting he can out-drink them."

Liz shakes her head. "Okay – so what happens?" The bartender places the drinks in front of Joe. He passes one to Liz.

"Well, he beats a lot of people, wins a lot of money. But then he goes back the next night, and this young girl in a red dress sits down next to him."

"You sure it wasn't a red miniskirt?" Liz tastes her new drink with the tip of her tongue. "Ugh. This is bad."

"You said something to warm you; it's whiskey." Joe takes a sip of his own drink. "So the girl comes into the bar wearing a red miniskirt."

Liz leans forward, places her hand on Joe's thigh. "And a white tube top."

"Yeah," Joe says. He takes her hand from his thigh, places it on the bar in front of her. He swallows his shot.

"Okay, honey. You tell it. I'll shut up." Liz runs her finger over her lips, pantomimes zipping and locking them and then tossing the key over her naked

73

Doug Frelke

shoulder. She puts her hand back on Joe's thigh; a little higher, a little further inside.

"Okay." Joe rubs his face, tries to remember his place. "So the girl in the red miniskirt and white tube top sits next to the lion tamer, and they start drinking tropical drinks – margaritas and daiquiris."

"Right." Liz lifts the shot glass, eyes the whiskey. She drinks it then, head back and poured right down her throat.

"Well, the girl starts to get hot – from the bar and all the drinking. By two AM, she stands up and drops her miniskirt to the floor. Then she sits back down at the table, and the lion tamer and the girl keep drinking. They order all kinds of mixed drinks: fuzzy navels, grasshoppers, sea breezes ..."

"How about flaming orgasms, slippery nipples, and sex on the beach?" Liz laughs.

Joe nods. "Sure." He lifts the already empty shot glass to his mouth. By the blue flight monitor, he sees he has twelve minutes to his flight. "At three in the morning, the girl decides she's still too hot. So she unbuttons her blouse, lays it on the table. That works for a while, and they go back to drinking. But by four, the girl is claiming she is even hotter still, on fire. So she takes off her bra and panties. Then she sits back down across from the lion tamer, completely naked."

Liz grins, "Hmm." She runs the tip of her tongue over her lips, pink over peach, in a wide, slow circuit. She moves her hand again, until it is full between Joe's legs.

"So all the drunks and the barflies and the working women have cut off their talk. They've fixed their eyes on the girl and the lion tamer. The girl stretches across the table, whispers in the lion tamer's ear. It's dead silent by then, and everyone can hear her say, 'If you put down your drink, we can go upstairs now.' And they all watch, as the lion tamer puts down his drink.

"Then he takes a long look at the girl – the way she stands there naked in the heat of the bar. And he says,

'No thanks. I don't think about love anymore. Because if I did, I might forget that lions have razor teeth. And those teeth would clamp down on my neck when I lay my head in the lion's mouth.'"

Liz removes her hand, leans back away from him. She is watching him from a new distance, and with the distance, Joe can see that she is sort of pretty even – with the tight skirt and her little tanned breasts and no fat at all, all muscle and bone.

"Why don't we go somewhere?" Liz says.

"I've got to catch my flight. Get home." Joe attempts to smile. "I couldn't afford your time."

Liz laughs. "Oh, there's a price, sure." Liz leans in to him, whispers, "but I'm pretty good, Joe. And I'll give you a rebate for that story of yours. That was something else."

Joe is silent then, and Liz leans back, waiting.

Joe reaches down for his duffel bag. Liz puts her hand on his wrist.

"Why don't you stop for awhile, Joe? You can always go home."

Joe looks at his watch, at the blue flight monitor, at the other people in the bar. He is thinking, trying to think. But the time is passing, five minutes more, then four, and then he will miss his flight home.

"No." And Joe stands then.

"Your choice." Liz smirks, and her wide mouth makes it awful.

"Sorry."

"Yeah. Me too." Liz sighs. "Give me your hand," she says.

Joe extends his hand and Liz takes it between both of hers, splaying out his fingers between her littler ones, lifts it close to her face. She turns his hand over, rubs his palm, kisses his fingertips.

She bites him then; deep in the soft skin between his thumb and index finger.

"Hell!" People in the bar turn to look; others moving past to their flights slow to focus on the two of

Doug Frelke

them.

Liz nods, as if she is agreeing with the people who stare at them. "Look at your hand, Joe."

A greasy peach smear runs from his thumb knuckle to the middle joint of his index finger; sharp, bluish dents dig a curve along both sides of his hand. "Feel that, Joe. You feel that. That's what it feels like to get bit." Liz picks up her drink. She moves over to the other end of the bar where a man in a blue blazer stands, watching the TV above him. "May I sit here?" she says, and he nods.

Joe picks up his duffel. Liz is saying something to the man, a whisper that the man leans down to hear. They both look at Joe and smile. Joe moves a few steps – a jog, a run. And he does not slow until he is on his plane, safely buckled in, with his duffel bag stowed under the seat in front of him.

"Where was I?" Past Marathon, Texas, Joe's eyes are caught by the klieg lights of the passing telephone poles. They are the only lights out here, lining the road; the rest is blackness, between the outstretched towns. Joe counts the poles in his head. His cousin's truck keeps moving, steady, cutting down the road between the telephone poles. He is twenty miles from home.

His cousin scratches his thinning head of red hair. Bobby is losing his hair, though he is almost five years younger than Joe. Joe knows Bobby is embarrassed about his hair, mainly due to the surprise of it – losing something he thought he had every right to.

"The girl had just left. The one with no clothes – she just walked out."

"Okay. So then the lion tamer looks around the room and announces, 'I'll give ten thousand dollars to any single man that can beat me.' And he takes out the money and lays it on the table."

Joe pats his pocket, takes out his empty cigarette pack. He crushes it with his left hand, drops it to the floor of the truck. "You got any cigarettes, cousin?"

Smoke

"No. I quit while you were in the Gulf."

Joe leans forward and opens the glove box. He shuffles through some papers, lifts out a flashlight, a wrench.

"If you find any in there, they'll be stale as hell, Joe." Bobby laughs. "I quit over two months ago."

Joe finds a pack, crumbled, wedged in the corner. He shakes out a few broken ones and tosses them through the open window. He lights a slightly bent whole one.

"It's stale, isn't it? Stale as hell. I told you."

"It's all right." Joe takes a long draw, props his head back on the seat. He lets the smoke trickle out of his mouth, gently, and it moves to the window in a steady line.

"Okay, so even with all the money, no one will take the lion tamer's bet. Finally, an old Apache Indian walks into the bar. He is wearing a loin cloth and a top hat; he looks like he's over a hundred years old. The Apache sits next to the lion tamer and says, 'I've heard all about you, Mr. Lion Tamer, and I'm a wise man, the wisest old Apache left in the world. I think I know how I can beat you,' and the Apache smiles a one-toothed grin. So the lion tamer orders whiskey and rum, and the game begins."

Bobby grimaces. "I like the part with the naked lady better than this. This part is kind of slow."

Joe stops. "Well, do you want to hear it?"

"Yeah, go on. I'm just saying."

"Anyway, the Apache builds up a big lead because he is wise and he has a magic system to help him keep his liquor. For the first time, the lion tamer looks like he might get beat. But then the Apache starts to slow, and the lion tamer pulls up even. The old Apache whispers in the lion tamer's ear, 'Young man, I have a deal for you. I am old, and I live on my reputation for being wise. I now see it was foolish of me to try and beat you. But I need to keep my reputation. So if you let me win, I'll tell you all of the great secrets of the

Doug Frelke

world; then, you can become wise like me, knowing everything.'"

Bobby rolls down his window and the wind pours into the cab then, blows the cigarette wrapper around the floor. "Hell, I need to clean this truck."

Joe nods. "But the lion tamer shakes his head and says, 'No deal.' The Apache doesn't understand; he thinks maybe he hasn't explained his offer clearly to the lion tamer. 'You will know everything, Mr. Lion Tamer. Why things happen the way they do in this world.'

"The lion tamer says, 'but you can't change a thing can you? Anymore than you can change the fact that I'm beating you. You're the wisest old Indian in the world and you know everything, but it all still happens.' And the lion tamer laughs, long and harsh. 'That's of no use to me, old man. When I'm in the ring, I don't think about money or love or knowing – I don't think at all. When I'm forcing my lions through the circle of fire, I can't be thinking about anything else. If I did, I might forget to remember that lions can leap. And then one of the lions would crush me.'"

Joe sticks his sore right hand out the window, lets the cool air run over its swolleness. "The lion tamer slaps the table. He says, 'You keep your secrets, you old fake, and get out.' And so the Apache gets up and shuffles off, leaves the lion tamer to drink by himself for awhile. And then, eventually, the lion tamer falls asleep."

"So he falls asleep after all that?"

"That's the story."

"Hell, I thought it would be a funny story, Joe. That kind of sucks." Bobby shifts in his seat, and the truck swerves a little, comes back to the middle of the lane.

Joe sits back, smokes. "It's a dumb story. Sorry."

Bobby wrinkles his forehead, but he doesn't say anything for awhile, just drives, and the wind keeps coming in, blowing bits of paper along the floor of the cab.

Smoke

Another pole flashes by and Joe adds it to his number. "I've got a list of things I want to do at the house. Put in an herb garden. Cut down the high grass behind the house and put in sunflowers. Pour a walk from the porch to the street."

"That will keep you busy."

"Yeah. I think so."

Bobby drives. He rubs his face, and Joe smiles then, watching him because he knows what his cousin is thinking. After a minute Bobby says, "Hey, let me have one of those cigarettes."

Joe laughs. "Here." He gives Bobby his own cigarette, lights another.

"To hell with you," Bobby says, but he smiles, too. He slows his truck and turns onto the dirt access road between the fields leading to the old house.

The house is solid and white; the headlights of Bobby's truck cut across the front yard and roll off into the fields behind the drive. The house has always been white as long as Joe can remember. It is his cousin's house now, but it was his Grandmother's house when Joe was a kid, and he and Bobby pretty much grew up there while their mothers went off and came back, went off and came back. Joe lived there until he joined the Navy and then he was married.

Bobby coughs from his cigarette. "This damn cigarette is stale."

"Yeah. You were right." The truck stops and Joe opens the door of the cab. Bobby lifts Joe's duffel from the back of his truck, slings it over his shoulder.

Up close, Joe can see that the house has been freshly painted – the porch, the rails, the wood steps. "Did you paint the house?"

"Yeah. Last week. I almost went with yellow; started it on the back. But it didn't look right, so I painted the whole thing over with the white."

"Yeah. It looks real good." Joe runs his bad hand, gently, over the rail.

"Bobby, what if I stayed here for awhile?"

79

Doug Frelke

"I thought you had things you wanted to do out at your place?"

"I do. I'm going to do them. Then I'll sell the place."

"Then what are you going to do?"

"I don't know, Bobby. I just thought of the first part, now as I got here." But Joe is happy. The clock has stopped ticking in his head. He is home.

"Come on, Joe," Bobby says, holding the front door open.

Joe nods to his cousin; but he does not go inside. Instead, Joe walks back down the porch steps, out past the truck, to the middle of the yard. He stands stock still and looks over the details of the old house – the sweep of the wooden porch, the spacing of the four paned windows, the line of the shingles along the roof.

El Corazon

Little Piece clipped his fingernails while he waited. He had opened early, by appointment – his blinds now up and his door unlocked. The cuttings made a small pile on his bench, and Little Piece double checked his work to make sure nothing escaped to dirty the floor. Then the tattooist took an emery board to each nail, checking twice for a jag or a split. He finished with a light dusting of the pads of his fingers to sharpen the feeling in the tips. He painted each nail gold and let them dry, adding a clear coat of vitamin E for strength.

The boy was supposed to be in at one.

The tattooist's real name was Thadeus Williams, but he was called Little Piece because he was small, in a shrunken, stunted way. He was black and known as a skilled renderer, a specialist who did good work on the darker skins. And the boy wanted something special, El Corazon. Little Piece was the only one in Perth who could make that rendering.

Little Piece was in his seventies, but looked older still, a kind of relic; you could smell the age of him, like old planks soaked in creosote and caulked with tar. He wore a gold hoop earring in his left ear because he was

Doug Frelke

a Navy legacy; he had been the one survivor when his destroyer, the *Alexander,* was sunk off the Australian coast. After Little Piece finished his tour, it was natural that he chose to stay on the beaches he had washed up on and he began to practice tattooing. The earring marked him, and the sailors who believed in luck went to him, since in their mind there was no greater luck than a true legacy. He was very popular; the sailors who didn't believe in luck also went to Little Piece, because he was smart enough to place his shop near the docks, right above the whorehouses and bars.

Little Piece heard the shift of his stairs, the old wood giving against someone's weight. "The boy," Little Piece thought. A Fillipino in uniform – an engineman was at his door, a card in his hand. Little Piece swept the nail bits into his hand and shook them into the trash. He blew on his nails, though the gold had been dry for some time.

The Filipino opened the door and came inside. He was small in the uniform – thin waisted, thick black hair. He did not look like an engineman – no muscles. And no dirt or grease ground into his skin.

The Filipino moved his eyes along the wall Little Piece had examples of all of his drawings there. Animals – tigers, wolves, cats, bears, snakes; cartoon characters and items of chance, like cards and dice. Little Piece had women on the wall, in every possible combination of color and size. In the far corner, there were even some Celtic weaves that Little Piece executed in India ink.

Little Piece saw the hair and thought the boy's ship must have been at sea for some time. Little Piece still remembered. Discipline was a little laxer on the long cruises; exceptions granted along the farther reaches.

"You said you wanted a heart."

The Filipino snapped his head from the wall. His eyes were sharp and wide, light brown to yellow irises, standing out from under his black hair. "Cat's eyes," thought Little Piece.

"On the phone. You said a Latino heart. I drew one for you. You the boy that called?" Little Piece asked but he knew.

"I called."

"Good, come look. See if this is what you want."

Little Piece framed his drawing with his long black fingers and the gilt of his nails. The design was El Corazon – a raw natural heart; so opposed to the cartoon-like valentine heart the North Americans favored. El Corazon was the real heart – blue veins and ventricles, as if Little Piece were drawing from a medical textbook.

He had spent most of the morning preparing the tracing; he had not done El Corazon in some time – close to two years. Little Piece remembered the first one he had drawn – twenty years before, a sailor from Ecuador. Little Piece remembered the man, his face a stone, heavy with scars. That man had requested the word "Bonita" under his heart, paying Little Piece with a leather pouch of silver dust.

"That's it."

"All right, sit down." Little Piece had his tools already prepared, laid out in a medical tray. "Take off the shirt."

The Filipino unbuttoned his shirt. He sat on the edge of the stool, his legs wrapped under him. He touched the right side of his chest. "Here."

Little Piece shook his head. "You don't want a tattoo on the chest, boy. It bleeds too much. Let me do the arm or the back. Those are good places."

"I want it where I say."

Little Piece frowned. "Then it will cost. It messes up my needles, all that blood."

"I will pay."

"Fine." Little Piece did not bother to argue. He would make it up in the price, and the boy would have to pay. He had been watching the boy's eyes since he had come into the shop – his eyes seemed so familiar to Little Piece – until finally, it came back to him in a quick breaking wave; they were the brown and yellow eyes of his old bunkmate from the *Alexander*.

Doug Frelke

Little Piece started the heart under the engineman's right nipple. He ran the pads of his fingers over the area, once, then twice, to feel the skin for any abnormalities that could harm his work — a scar, a vein, an irregular mole. But the skin was smooth, young and unmarked. He rubbed his fingers over the area once more.

He started his machine. A high-pitched whirr rose and fell as the needles worked, not unlike the sound of a high speed drill. Most of his customers hated the sound. But the engineman seemed to relax — his skin slackened, his chest moved more slowly in and out. "Let's go," he said.

Little Piece painted a deep red vein, a bright unreal red that stood out sharply against the flow of the Filipino's dark blood.

"Invisible skin," Little Piece thought. Veins drawn over veins and hearts beside hearts.

As the tattooist cut, the Filipino bled. When the flow became too heavy, Little Piece would stop and wipe away the blood with a paper towel so he could see his work. Little Piece tossed the dirty towels in the trashcan; when the basket was full, he dropped them on the old wood floor.

The Filipino did not flinch, nor did he speak. Once when Little Piece cut too deep, he scowled, but only once. Then, just a vacant face again, and those cat eyes searching every movement of Little Piece's hand, as if expecting some form of betrayal.

When he was sure the design was finished, Little Piece salved and bandaged the Filipino's chest. His face had gone close to white under the fluorescent lights. The Filipino had bled more than Little Piece would have liked, but the tattoo was a fine thing. It had been easy once Little Piece could trust that the boy would not move.

He offered the boy some of his beer, and they drank for a while and talked. Little Piece watched the beer slowly bring the color back to the Filipino's face. He

El Corazon

remembered his bunkmate's name had been Francis, but they had called him Cisco because he was born in that town. He had perfect teeth; white and unchipped, and Little Piece had liked to take the tip of his finger and run it over Cisco's lips, slipping in to touch the edges of those perfect teeth.

They had been together when the ship commenced its final rolls, climbed the last few yards from the berthing stairwell to the open deck. And Little Piece had hit Cisco twice, then three times, then four, his fist clutching a marlinespike, smashing those teeth and wresting away the last life preserver on the *Alexander*.

"Why the heart?" Little Piece shook his empty can of beer and lowered it to the floor. "Love?"

The engineman leaned back in his chair. "For love. For luck."

"How luck?" Little Piece had written a thousand words of love and carved at least as many charms. He pointed his gold tipped finger at the engineman. "A heart is love."

The boy shrugged. "Love then."

After about an hour, Little Piece cleared his throat. He said, "You owe me two hundred dollars."

"Too much." The Filipino finished his beer and placed the can on the floor, as Little Piece had done.

Little Piece knew the price was a half a month's pay for an engineman. A very high price. He nodded. "That is a lot of money for you to have to pay."

"I have it." The engineman's eyes caught Little Piece's gold nails, watched them move from his beer can to his lips. The boy did not reach for his wallet.

"Good," Little Piece said. "But maybe a hundred is more fair. For a friend."

The engineman got up from the chair. He shook his black haired head. "Friends," he said. He took another of Little Piece's beers and opened it. He carried it with him to the rear of the shop.

The tattooist crossed to his door and locked it. He brought his blinds down, one then the other. No one

Doug Frelke

should come by this early. If they did, they would knock and he would be able to hear them, even from the room in back. He would not be that long.

"So tell us the story, Mcauley." Fontaine leaned back against the wall on the main control booth. The engines ran loud, still warming to their best speed. Fontaine kept his good eye on the gauges, watching for signs that the days of idle had caused any trouble. The booth was cramped with three men inside. Fontaine was the only one seated. He was a first class engineman and it was his watch. The other engineman, Kantala, had his shirt off, exposing the grey patch of gauze covering his fresh tattoo.

Fontaine had a lazy eye, and he used it to effect, letting it float back and forth across Mcauley. Mcauley was a topside sailor, bosunmate – Fontaine had called him down to talk. And he had called him down into the engines, among the enginemen, to answer a question about how one of the other enginemen had been badly beaten while on liberty.

Fontaine sat back on a stool in the middle of the booth, facing aft and looking out at his engines: One and Three Main on his left, Two and Four on his right. Three sides of the booth and the door into the space were Plexiglas; the one solid wall was behind Fontaine, divided by a brass escape ladder leading to the upper decks. Kantala leaned against the throttles. The bosunmate, Mcauley, stayed near the door.

"Yeah, so how did it happen?" Fontaine ran his hand over the two days of beard on his face.

"I already told it to the Master at Arms. Ask him, Fontaine."

"I figure you'd tell it better."

Mcauley spit on the floor. "How come he isn't wearing his shirt?"

"I just got a tattoo," Kantala said.

Mcauley laughed. "Yeah, that's good. I got six." Mcauley rolled up his sleeves. "See these two?"

El Corazon

Mcauley had a white blond girl and a black red headed girl, each inked on one of his biceps. "I got them here – four years ago."

Kantala looked at the designs. "I heard you were the one that got Garcia. Because he was a fag."

Mcauley did not speak.

Fontaine shook his head. "Did I ever tell you I caught him down here once, with one of the shipyard birds? It was in Brisbane. A goddamn Sri Lankan. I don't think the yard bird could even speak English."

"I don't know what the fuck he was." Mcauley scratched his arms. He was sunburned from falling asleep on the beach. "Goddamned and unnatural."

"Yeah." Fontaine rubbed his wide flat nose. He was white but he had come from New Orleans. The mulatto blood was still thick in him, marking his face and the kink of his hair. "They say you broke Garcia's head wide open at the Fiddler."

Kantala nodded. "They say you used a beer bottle, and his head cracked like an egg shell."

Mcauley's mouth opened, closed. He said, "Yeah. Garcia was making passes at me. Garcia wanted to suck my dick, okay? Wanted me to go behind the bar with him, into the alley. So I went. And I busted him when I got there." Mcauley wiped his mouth. "I didn't know his head would split like that."

Fontaine rocked in his chair. "See, we heard different, I guess."

Kantala thrust his head under the forced draft blower, rotating slowly. He removed the bandage, exposing the bruised and bloody design to the air. "Like you had been asking him."

Almost like he was washing himself, Mcauley thought. Like a goddamn cat. Still, Mcauley knew about tattoos. He figured Kantala's had probably scabbed up overnight, and now the tattoo had begun to itch. Mcauley remembered the itch – at first it was nothing, but it quickly became a layered pain that had no ebb to it, always racheting up a notch.

Doug Frelke

"That's bullshit, Fontaine. The Master at Arms cleared me. Everyone knew Garcia was a faggot."

Kantala turned to Mcauley; his eyes made the hull technician nervous. "That's what a faggot gets."

"Yeah. That's what a dick sucking faggot gets." Mcauley balled his fists. "And I'd do it again."

Fontaine laughed. "See we had heard different. But I guess that's fine then." Fontaine leaned back with his stool, making room for Mcauley to open the door. "Thanks for clearing that up."

"Sure. I just wanted to make it clear. I got no problem with the enginemen."

"You made it clear. No problems." Fontaine nodded. "Kantala, go wipe down Number Three. Let me know if she's leaking any oil."

"Sure," said Kantala.

When Mcauley had been gone awhile, Kantala said, "I want Mcauley blued."

Fontaine smiled. "I figured."

"I saved a hundred dollars."

"Good, it will take that. I'll get two of the black Muslims to do it. That way, the Master at Arms will think it's a race thing." Fontaine put his face next to the Plexiglas, so his one good eye could focus on the numbers along the control panel. "Plus, getting to hurt a white Irish prick like Mcauley – they may do it cut rate."

"Fine, you know how to do it."

"Yep." Fontaine nodded. "You know what they do?"

"I don't need to know – I just need it done."

"Sure. I got that. But you should know." Fontaine watched the engines, gauge by gauge. He thought – he doesn't know and he doesn't want to know, but that's the price of doing it.

"It's like getting raped, only instead of fucking him, they smack his balls with the bluing. It will stain him for about three months."

Kantala used a rag on the throttles, polishing the numbered knobs. "Good. That's what I want."

"All right." Fontaine focused his good eye. "If

Mcauley thinks it was you, he might split your head, too."

Kantala gingerly reset the bandage. "Let him come."

"And hope you are lucky." Fontaine laid his ear against the wall – the engines were warming into gear, beginning to balance – he could hear numbers One, Two, and Three slide into their normal timing. "Nice tattoo." The tape of the bandage had separated from Kantala's skin. The bandage flagged in the blower air.

"Garcia had one like that, a Spanish heart. What do they call it?"

"El Corazon. They call it El Corazon."

"Sure they do." Fontaine squinted out into the space. "Hell, I can't see. Go check the temps on number Four. She seems to be having a tough time warming up."

Kantala put on his shirt. He grabbed a rag from the corner and headed out into the heavy heat of the space, and all its noise and motion and grease.

Sophia Bonita

Billy warns me. "Keep your beer in your hand – she'll sit on it." But I barely hear him – I'm thinking more about a cold beer and how good the darkness feels, walking into the bar and out of the hundred and ten degree Tijuana heat. Anyway, I can't see a damn thing, going from the bright sun to blackness, but we just walk in like blind men, our hands out in front and taking baby steps.

They're playing honky tonk, Waylon Jennings and Hank Williams, and I just move towards the music until my eyes start to come back to me. I see Billy peel over to the bar to get us some drinks. The place had been a cinema at one time, with the bar near the door and the rest of the room slanted down about a hundred feet to a stage backed by a twenty foot red velvet curtain with black lettering, "Velvet Cowgirl." A few Mexicans line the concrete walls, smoking and talking in small clots under the noise of the music.

"We're early," Billy says, and hands me my two Coronas, and we walk down to the edge of the stage. Billy has been to the Velvet Cowgirl before, and I trust Billy – we've been working together at UPS for about a

Sophia Bonita

year, and he helped me out when I first started, kept me from being a stiff that worked too hard. Billy let me in on a few tricks, like how to dog it a little without getting the supervisor pissed off. He knows about things. Like about the stage show.

Billy removes his cowboy hat and brushes his crew cut with his fist. "Wait until you see Sophia. She's like Babe Ruth or Mohammed Ali. She's that big down here."

After about five minutes, a white guy comes down the aisle and sits next to us. He's American, too. His name is Donnie and he's a strange fish – awfully thin and long white hair like Johnny Rivers. He looks like an albino, wearing big black Raybans over his eyes. When he takes off the glasses, I see he has blue eyes, instead of pink little albino eyes, but he's really torched from the sun – the skin is peeling off in strips around his white eyebrows.

Donnie is talking about his job, but I can't quite get the gist of it other than it is basically illegal, because Donnie keeps saying, loudly, how fucking smart you have to be – doing what he's doing. I know anybody with eyes like that has just come in from a trip through the desert – their first trip, since no one would ever do that to themselves twice. But I try to be polite by just ignoring him.

About forty Mexicans from the concrete plant come in, laughing and shouting amongst themselves. Some Mexican whores come in too, mixed in with the workers, and they start hustling the floor of the Velvet Cowgirl trying to make follow-on dates. The whores target the young guys. "Boyfriend," they coo, and speak in little Spanish phrases that sound like pretty strings of glass beads. The older workers pretend to be jealous, taunting the young men to accept the girls' offers. The pimps lean against the pink concrete walls watching the girls work, sometimes yelling at a girl they think isn't really trying. Still, everyone seems to be in a good mood, the Mexican construction guys, the

Doug Frelke

whores and the pimps – all of us settling into the red velvet and waiting for the show to start.

The country music gets a quick cut, and the DJ says something, possibly in English but I can't make it out. A new record scratches over the stereo system, and then the start of *Bolero*. Then the whole back row of pimps erupts, screaming "Sophia!" The concrete workers join in, banging the armrests of their seats. Billy, Donnie, and me start screaming too – real loud because we don't want the Mexicans to think Americans can't make as much noise as them.

The curtain never parts. Instead, the music keeps ripping for about two minutes and then she sort of trundles out. Sophia. She wears a red velvet wrap over her G-string and pasties, and she is old and fat. I mean really old for this line of work – like late fifties, maybe even sixty. She looks like a cleaning lady; maybe that is her day job up in San Diego. And she is stone drunk, too – barely standing, with a huge dumb smile nailed to her face.

I look at Donnie and Billy, ready to leave, but Billy seems to be enjoying it and Donnie is eye-balling the whores at the back of the room.

The music changes then, goes low and slow, with a black woman singer. Sophia drops the wrap behind her and bends over to pull off her high heels. As she bends, one of the concrete workers yells, "Sophia Bonita!" She looks out towards the sound and blows a kiss. The rest of the workers laugh. I laugh too – it's funny the way she does it, like she knows she is fat and old and yet the Mexican guy really meant it.

I think of my mother. Which I guess is kind of sick in a way, but mostly I'm thinking about when my step-dad and her took me to Las Vegas to see Elvis. I was nine, and they told me what a big deal Elvis was. And I could see they that were both excited, even my step-dad, who was a big geek ex-marine and normally boring as hell.

When I saw Elvis, he was just a fat guy in a bad

Sophia Bonita

polyester suit who didn't even seem to know all the words to his songs. But my mom saw someone different. There was a point in the show where Elvis throws out silk scarves – he touches one to his forehead, kisses it, throws the scarf to the audience. When he did that, the whole place went nuts. My own mother, with her support hose and her varicose veins, went nuts. And she got one of those damn scarves, too, pushed her way right to the front and left me and my step-dad at the table. She cried like a baby over it two years later when she heard Elvis had died.

Without the heels, Sophia is better – you can tell this is how she likes to dance – barefoot and naked. She smiles; just a little thin smile, not like the big fake one in her opening, but a sign she is enjoying herself, she knows she's showing us something. She still isn't great, but she's good and someone in the back starts clapping, and the rest of us take it up until she is dancing to the hand beaten claps, not the music from the speakers.

And I start to see it – hints of what she must have been like ten, twenty, thirty-five years back. She would look at you, single you out, and you know she is dancing to get you, just you, no expression on her face because she's moving up a hill somewhere, moving to a summit and carrying you along. And I go along, the Mexicans go along, almost everyone did.

Donnie yawns. He says, "This is bullshit. I'm bored."

He says it like a sneak, just to me and Billy. He puts his beer on the edge of the stage, and points to the back of the room. "Let's move to the back and chase a few of the whores."

So Donnie doesn't see her. At first, I think I'm the only one who catches it, Sophia is so smooth, but when I look around the room everyone is laughing, the whores, the pimps, Billy – they all know the joke.

Donnie turns back around, to me. "What, what did I miss? What?" He slides his Raybans down his nose,

93

Doug Frelke

squints back at the stage. The pimps and the construction workers begin to shout, "bebe!" in strangled gasps, pointing at Donnie and lifting their own beers in pantomime.

"They want you to drink," I say.

Donnie looks at Billy, but Billy can't speak, he's laughing so hard. He just nods, pointing at Donnie's beer.

"Fuck the whole gang of you," Donnie says, and then he picks up his beer and takes a long cool sip, just like he has to.

There is a wild sound then, ripe and free, deafening. But I am looking at Sophia. She is dancing. And what can I say, but I am killed in love. Sophia Bonita.